Also available in Large Print
by Mary McMullen:

Better Off Dead
The Other Shoe

A
Grave Without
Flowers

A Grave Without Flowers

MARY McMULLEN

G.K. HALL & CO.
Boston, Massachusetts
1984

Published in Large Print by arrangement with
Doubleday & Company, Inc.

Set in 16 pt English Times.

Library of Congress Cataloging in Publication Data

McMullen, Mary, 1920-
  A grave without flowers.

  "Published in large print"—T.p. verso.
  1. Large type books. I. Title.
[PS3563.A31898G7 1983b]   813'.54   84-4521
ISBN 0-8161-3704-8

To Alton

A
Grave Without
Flowers

ONE

"Where's your girl Luce?" Jonesy cast an eye up the crowded bar at Gullion's pub. "In hiding?"

"Hiding from what?" Denis Taunton asked. After thirstily attacking his pint of bitter, he added, "It's her day off."

"Not so much from what as from who. I was thinking about Tickell."

"Tickell? Oh—her jailhouse boyfriend." Denis's wanderings had taken him, among other places, to the southern United States and an occasional regional Americanism flavored his casually well-bred speech. "Is he sprung?"

"This week, I hear."

"Well, after four years or so, he'd hardly expect her to be wrapped up in white gift paper and pink ribbon waiting for him?"

"Maybe not . . . but they've been on-again off-again ever since she was fifteen. You might call her his second home. He was living at her place

1

when they picked him up. I suppose at the least he'd go back there to collect his things."

"And I'm to worry about him? Or she is?"

"I just thought I'd mention it." Jonesy sipped his lager thoughtfully. "He has, or used to have, a triggery kind of temper. Not that he ever let it loose in Brixton. Good as gold, I hear. Which is why they shaved a couple of years off his sentence."

Handy, when you come to think of it, Denis said to himself. Not that he needed a Tickell to help him compose his exit lines, but it might make Luce feel a little better: a reason for, after seven months with her, calling it quits.

Their battle last night, over a girl at the bar Luce considered he'd looked too interested in, had very little to do with it. He had for several weeks been feeling the familiar pull of the unseen magnet. Time to move on. Luce—past tense—had been great fun.

She had gone off this morning, still in a huff, to spend the day at Florian's House of Beauty, where her friend Nanette worked. Nanette would give her the works at half price, mudpack, massage, shampoo, styling cut, and God knows what else. She availed herself of Nanette's amiable services once every four or five weeks. He was still in bed when she left the flat at nine. That is, he was on the couch, where after their quarrel she had hurled a sheet and a pillow. Going out the door, she had said, "Expect me when you see me. Late."

2

Good. It was only a bit past seven now.

He finished his pint and in a decisive way slapped the mug down on the bar. "See you, Jonesy." He opened Gullion's heavy oak door inset with ovals of etched glass and went out into the thin cold drizzle of the June evening.

A swift four-block walk brought him to Kennan's Gold Star Car-Hire. Joe Kennan was in his office on the second floor of the garage at the rear, where the good cars—the two Rollses, the Daimlers, the Bentleys, and the custom-built Gaspard—were kept protected from the elements.

On seeing his visitor's ascending dark head and broad shoulders in the stairwell, Kennan produced a bottle of whiskey from a desk drawer.

"No thanks," Denis said.

"Right and proper. Drivers oughtn't to be drinkers." Kennan poured three fingers for himself. "That is, if—are you taking me up then?"

He had called late yesterday with the offer of a job. Denis had driven for him before and was not only reliable but had that mysterious dash of class which made him, for the occasional special job, the first man to come to mind.

"Two women, Americans, want to do a tour of the National Trust gardens. They'd need you for a minimum of two weeks, maybe a little over. How about it?"

Yesterday, Denis hadn't been very interested. He still had some money in his pocket from a spell of tree work at the Gorhams' in Sussex,

3

topping poplars along the half-mile drive and moving a chrysanthemum garden Mrs. Gorham had decided would look nicer down by the stream. But that was yesterday.

"What sort of women are they?" He had once done a job for Kennan, driving a Mrs. Bledsoe, who had a broken ankle, from London to Edinburgh. She had turned amorous halfway there and when he failed to evidence any response she had leaned over from the back seat and hit him on the head with a half-full bottle of port. Fortunately, they had stopped for a red light.

"I only saw one of them. She came by to choose a car herself. The Gaspard, by the way, even though I warned her it drinks petrol like champagne. Very nice lady, a Mrs. Wallace."

"Okay. When and where?"

After Kennan gave him his instructions and settled with him about what he was to be paid, Denis took the Underground to Southwark and walked to the shabby brick house on Call's Lane where Luce's flat was. As promised, or threatened, it was empty. He got out his duffle bag, packed his clothes, and cast a quick glance about for loose possessions.

Dark glasses, a pair of sandals half under the bed, toothbrush, comb, a bottle of aspirin he'd paid for, three new paperbacks he'd bought last week. The cigarette case? Why not, she'd given it to him, and one way or another it might turn out to be valuable.

He wrote a brief note and left it on the kitchen

table propped against a pot of bony geraniums with yellowing leaves. "Luce, I'm off. I've very much enjoyed the spin with you. Luck in everything, and take care. Denis."

Soften it, blur it a little? "P.S. I understand a very old friend may be rejoining you, so it ought to work out all around. D."

TWO ❧ ❧ ❧

"What we are about to see is Brow Hall, built in
... mmm ... mmm ..." Flora said, consulting
her notes. " 'The Pear Walk is very fine,
culminating as it does in the garden temple laden
with the thousand flowers of Rosa Brunonii
casting its fragrance in a sumptuous fashion ...
the heliotrope circle in a clearing in the woods
with its fountain by ...' " Her musing voice
changed pitch. "I'll thank you, Leo, to leave my
heel alone!"

The seven-month-old apricot toy poodle at her
feet paid no attention to this order and Flora
picked him up to kiss his head, the better to
discipline him.

Denis, at the wheel, regarded her in the driving mirror with detached amusement. Flora Wallace, Mrs. Reginald Wallace, late forties he
thought, rich, he gathered—considering the petrol-
swallowing large Gaspard they were traveling in,

the magnificent Fortnum and Mason willow hamper in its boot, the ease and amplitude of her arrangements as displayed on their, so far, two and a half days on the road.

But not giving much of a damn about her appearance, which of course was a privilege of the rich. Her thick untidy hair was dyed an unlikely shade of red. Her lipstick looked as if she had put it on in the dark. Her features were strong, but slightly crooked. Her powerfully blue gaze could be commanding, or alternatively soft and kind. Her clothing was of a highly individual nature. Today, a loose shin-length dress made of squares of pink and tan crochet-work joined together by maroon leather whip-lacings. With a hat, its ruffled brim making it a species of mob-cap, to match. He had heard her tell Emily Denver when they had started out this morning, "An old friend—I don't believe you've ever met Eulalia?—made this for me. Unusual, wouldn't you say?"

"Very unusual," agreed Emily.

Leo wriggled out of Flora's embrace and crossed several feet of the tapestry-upholstered, sofa-pillowed back seat of the Gaspard to try out the comforts of Emily's lap.

"A dog?" Emily had asked in mild dismay when she had arrived in London a week after Flora got there. "In a car?"

"I couldn't resist him, and I'm never quite happy without a dog," Flora had explained. "He's championship stock, although he doesn't look *quite* . . . but that's perhaps why I fell for him so. The Dinnotsons breed them, you know." She had stayed at the Dinnotsons' in Yorkshire while waiting for Emily.

The two women had met three years ago in the lobby of the Algonquin Hotel in New York, where Emily was waiting for a writer she was going to take to lunch and Flora was waiting for her husband. Flora sat pursuing her sport of people watching and finally turned her gaze to the occupant of the next chair. Quiet, youngish, brown-haired, her face (although Emily didn't see this in her own mirror) shadowed with loss and loneliness. She was reading a small blue-bound Oxford University Press edition of Trollope's *Can You Forgive Her?*

On impulse, Flora said, "I didn't know anyone read Trollope anymore. I adore him. I have that whole set, Oxford, except that someone borrowed my copy of *Phineas Finn* and never returned it."

They fell easily into talking about books. Emily was an editor with the publishing house of Faunt and Faunt. Her writer guest was late, Flora's husband, Reginald, had been caught in a traffic jam, and the conversation continued. They had been fast friends ever since.

Flora learned, in a roundabout unembellished way, the reason for the shadow of loss on the narrow face. A recent divorce, not quite yet assimilated. The usual, Flora gathered: another woman. Emily did not enlarge upon the other woman.

8

There was ten years' difference in their ages—Emily was then thirty-one—but their relationship was easy, warm, comfortable, and undemanding. They lived not far from each other; Emily in a new small unmemoried apartment she had fled to after the divorce, the Wallaces in a fourteen-room duplex in what had been the Vandever mansion, across the street from the Metropolitan Museum.

Summers, Emily usually spent two or three long weekends at the Wallaces' country place in the Poconos, shaking the dust of publishing out of her system.

In her kind and she hoped unobtrusive way, Flora looked about for men, or more properly the one right man for Emily.

It seemed to her it would have to be a very special kind of man. Emily had, to her friend's discerning eye, or nose, a potpourri quality, a fragrance of the being. A tender suggestion of rose petals, an edge of spice, an occasional witty sting of citrus peel. Her intelligence worn softly, her personal grace a light and delicate garment.

And now that there seemed to be one among her sought-out possibilities about to work out permanently for Emily, Flora was not so sure. Otis Hale, a partner in Reginald's law firm. Nice, but. Attractive in his rosy solid way, but. Financially safe and sound, but. One divorce, years ago, no children to complicate matters, but.

"I need yeast in my dough," Otis had confided to Flora. "I need Emily."

There were as yet no definite marriage plans. Perhaps in the fall, Emily had said without any great certainty to Flora. Which was one of the reasons why Flora had decided to embark on a journey she had had at the back of her mind for years: a tour of fabled English gardens. With, now, Emily as her companion and insofar as Emily would allow it, her guest. Sometimes matters viewed from across an ocean had a way of putting themselves in their proper perspectives.

"I don't know," Emily had said when invited. "With what's happening in the world, things getting darker . . . and grimmer, and closer . . . it seems such a frivolous thing to do. An other-century thing to do. Old gardens. And straw hats with ribbons on them."

"A few weeks away from the troublesome scene won't change *it* and may help cheer you up," Flora said. "And I do want and need your company. I can't imagine anyone else I know who'd be so little bother, wandering along pleached alleys and around walled roseries. Reg can't get away to go anywhere until December, and he's inclined to think that when you've seen one garden you've seen them all."

"All right," Emily said, and on this June forenoon pouring gold among green trembling shadows was pleased that she had. Delighted that she had.

Flora was still deep in her notes, inscribed by her from various sources in a student's composition book of the Woolworth variety, with mottled black-and-white covers. It was a somewhat disorganized affair; every time Flora picked it up folded maps fell out, along with unattached slips of scribbled-over paper. "Let's see, eleven forty-five," she said with a glance at her watch. "We don't want to do Brow Hall on an empty stomach. When you find a nice tree, or grove, to park under, Denis—and Leo needs walking any second now."

Around a curve a great roadside beech presented itself. The grass verge was broad and silky. Denis came around to open the verge-side door, leashed Leo, and with the leash hooked over his forearm went to the boot. He took from it an immense striped Hudson's Bay wool blanket and the willow hamper. Emily spread the blanket on the grass while Denis started down the road with the tugging Leo.

There was something, Emily thought, endearingly luxurious, romantic and bygone, about picnic hampers, especially one like this. The lid now hospitably thrown back, it showed its lining of blue-and-white French gingham, its strapped-in Wedgwood plates and cups and saucers, its cutlery and crystal and gingham napkins, and its promising burden of good things to eat. There was a deep side pocket to keep things hot, another to keep things cold, each under the control of unseen batteries.

"Hot tea or—I think it's a day for chilled white wine," Flora said. "I'm sure it's all right for Denis, we'll be at Brow Hall in no time, and he'll have two hours or so to clear his head—if, that is, it affects him in any way. He looks like a man with a good capacity. I think we are quite lucky in Denis, don't you?"

"I feel right now that we are quite lucky in everything," Emily said contentedly. She sipped her white wine, breathed air afloat with summer scents, and watched Flora spreading caviar on thin golden toast taken from the hot pocket. "Oh, butterflies," she announced like a happy child as a little white dance began overhead.

"Cabbage butterflies," Flora amended. "A great trial if you're raising cabbages, but quite pretty otherwise. Ah, Denis—just in time, while your toast is still warm. You do drink wine?"

"Yes indeed." He put an openly protesting Leo into the car and took an approving taste from his Waterford wine glass. The three sat comfortably disposed on the blanket, eating their caviar toast and drinking their Reisling. Not for the first time, Emily found herself intrigued by Denis's blend of courtesy and efficiency (this man for hire) with ease in himself and with his employers.

He was a very tall man, a good three or four inches over six feet, slim, strong and well made. He had a classically modeled face with a high brow, large clear blue eyes, an outward and upward jut to his chin, and a long columnar neck a woman might well envy. His nose was boldly cut, his dark hair strongly waving about his ears and over his forehead. He wore a self-contained compromise between uniform and non-uniform, a dark roll-neck jersey and navy blue drill pants.

Emily had decided in a tentative fashion that there was nothing, after all, mysterious about him. He was a certain kind of contemporary young man, not wanting the office, the buttoned-up life, the reassurance of the salary to balance the boredom. Preferring freedom, work as you go, turn a hand to this, to that, pick up a skill here and there, and don't worry a great deal where you'll sleep tomorrow or next week, or what and when you'll eat and drink.

Which probably accounted for the faint impression she occasionally got: adventurer? or amiable rogue?

There was a sharp plaintive barking from inside the car. Leo's nose had been steadily pressed to the window, his dark eyes beadily watching each bite of food being consumed. "Just as soon as we finish our peaches," Flora called to him.

Denis took them smoothly through the bustling traffic of the town of Brow. "I don't know this part of the country," he said, "or I'd use the back roads."

"That's all right, you do have an imperious way with other cars," Flora said.

He smiled. "It's not me, it's the Gaspard."

He was a driver so skilled that even Emily's Manhattan nerves didn't twitch. When proposing the journey, Flora had said, "We won't drive ourselves. That's no way to *see* things. Trying to get used to the left side of the road, and worrying about running over chickens or being caught behind a team of horses hauling a cart of manure . . . on a hot sunny day. And I seem to recall, Emily, that like most clever and highly imaginative people you're no prize at the wheel.''

Their garden stops had already fallen into a pattern. Denis stayed behind, reading his paperback in the car and taking Leo for strolls. Emily and Flora went their own ways, following their own eyes and noses. Flora carried an innocent-looking straw basket, lidded, in which reposed a pair of sharp scissors, a tiny V-headed trowel, clippers, a supply of damp peat moss, and plastic bags and envelopes of various sizes.

Yesterday, catching her illicitly at work at Sissinghurst, swiftly troweling up a snippet of pinks including a bit of root, she had said, ''Flora! You're running the risk of arrest, trial, and very possibly hanging.'' ''Nonsense,'' said Flora. ''Most things can use thinning, it gives them more air to breathe. And these are—I forget the name, but you can't get them at home, even ordering from Wayside.'' She added, ''Anyway, no one but you spotted me.'' ''Well, I never knew gardening could make felons out of people,'' Emily said.

Wandering off by herself, she was surprised again by the way the mind emptied itself in a great garden and the senses were allowed, joyously, to take over. She had a taste for small, hidden, secret things and found in a copse of airy maidenhair trees a slender little stream, its edges thick with dwarf lilies. Following it—and to

14

devote yourself to following a stream to see where it went seemed the most delightful thing in life—she found to her joy that it now became a musical miniature waterfall into a rock pool jeweled with the dartings of goldfish.

She sat down at the edge of the pool to watch the goldfish, and tickled the water with three fingers to see if one of them might come to her. There was no sound except for the water, falling, and a breezy murmuring of the maidenhair branches overhead.

"Emily," said a man's voice behind her. The voice speaking one word, here in this remote place, this dream of green, had the effect on her of a crash of cymbals.

Crash of the heart too, painful and for the moment snatching away breath. As she tried to leap upright her foot slipped on a patch of moss and she almost fell. He reached out a steadying hand.

Bad enough, the shock of the voice. Worse, the shock of the hand, the remembered flesh and bone.

"Robert."

Don't say anything ridiculous, obvious. But she did. "What on earth are you doing here?"

"I might ask the same of you," he said. "Mentally, I had you sitting in your office at—what is it called now, the way the giants are buying up publishing houses, Subsidiary and Sons Incorporated? And here you are at Brow Hall trying to catch goldfish."

15

He might have been watching her silently for a moment, or minutes, tickling the surface of the water with her fingers. Unnerving small thing added to a general dropping-out of the bottom of your world.

"I'm doing a garden tour, not an official group tour but a . . . that is, we are—you don't know her—" Emily heard her verbal lurching and hated herself for it. Perhaps if she stopped looking directly into his eyes, a dark tea-colored hazel, with the thin white scar down the center of one eloquent ruddy eyebrow. Too sudden, too close, and too much, the eyes.

She dropped her glance to his cleft chin. "I'm spending my vacation sniffing pinks and admiring delphiniums," she said. "With a friend, Flora Wallace, whom I met," make it firm, make it calm, "right after we parted company."

Oddly enough—in a jet-shrunk world and still with a friend or two in common—they had not encountered each other since the divorce.

He was, she gathered, a success in his own way, writing and directing films, taking his time with them, sometimes wandering from country to country to make them. Not great X- or PG-rated smashes, but the off-center, the fresh and exploratory. Or so the critics said; she had not chosen to undergo a blast of Robert's work on a theater screen with hundreds and hundreds of people around her. During the four years of their marriage, he had been in a way training for this work, in New York, free-lancing television scripts

16

for a long-running and unexpectedly distinguished series, "Cityscape."

He had said he was too basically lazy and frivolous to contemplate working at home, at their apartment, and had found a modest studio room setup on Barrow Street in the Village. It was there that they—he and Vera Moore . . . there that they . . .

THREE ❧ ❧ ❧

Long after Robert hit his stride with his scripts for "Cityscape" and was making a great deal of money, he kept his shabby little studio on Barrow Street.

In the last three or four months of their marriage, not-quite-right months but Emily didn't then know why, she said that as he was making pots and that as her money wasn't bad either they might move to a larger apartment, so that he could have his own studio-office on the premises. It would be nice, she said—meaning only kindness, and love, and the great pleasure of having him near—nicer for both of them.

He had given her a strange sharp look and said in a voice unlike his own, "I'm better off the leash, Emily." And then, at her startled pink flush, "No, I don't mean that. It's just that I work better with no interesting distractions but the view out of my very dirty window."

18

"All right, stay in your monk's cell, then," Emily said. She'd been there only once or twice; she was fastidious about intruding on the privacy of concentrated work, the lonely work of the writer.

But when it began, several nights each week, his not coming home at all, she worried about his getting enough rest. Sometimes, he said, the oiled wheels started turning at say six or seven in the evening and he'd work until two or three in the morning.

She recalled with dismay the couch in the office, an ancient cracked leather couch with all the springs broken in the center cushion. After a few hours of sleep snatched on that monster, no wonder that the next day he looked tired and pale, withdrawn. And emotionally unapproachable.

No matter how valuable his professional freedom is to him, Emily told herself sternly, this amounts on my part to downright neglect. His birthday was coming up, an appropriate time to see to his health and comforts. She went to Bloomingdale's and bought a twin-size boxspring and mattress. To the amazement and dismay of the furniture salesman, she ordered both pieces gift-wrapped and sent to the Barrow Street address. "That will cost you considerable, madam," the salesman said. "I don't believe we've ever gift-wrapped bedding before." "Perfectly all right," Emily said. "I'll just write a note for you to tuck into the ribbon somewhere." Delivery in about a week, the salesman told her.

Her note said, "When you must sleep away from me, sweet dreams, my darling Robert."

And then on to the linens department for sheets, pillow, geranium-red blanket, throw-cover for daytime of quilted gray. Although, thought Emily, he'll probably never make up the bed. But while you're at it, do it right—the works.

"Please be sure," she said to the saleswoman, "that this goes out in the same delivery with the bed I just bought upstairs," and waited to see the notation, involving a lot of numbers, made on the salescheck.

It would take months, years, a small eternity to get through the privately blushing rage and shame, the pain of that happy day's gift-shopping.

It wasn't a week but nine days later when she got, at eleven in the morning in her office at Faunt and Faunt, the call from Robert.

"Thanks ever so much for your present, Emily."

How could a man, your husband, your love, sound like an icy stranger, or a human flame thrower, both at once—or at *all?*

She could find no voice to answer him.

"But you didn't, you know, need to spend all that money and go to all that trouble. Could you really have thought we always had to make do with the spavined old couch here? Our alternative bed is quite roomy and comfortable." He paused on a choking sound.

20

Emily sat, trembling, in a vacuum in which there was no feeling or comprehension of any kind. She would have to, when her mind started up again, go back and listen to these words and hear and understand them, identify them, make them into a meaning. A statement.

"I . . ." I what? Nothing. Her ears were ringing. Was he saying something or was that just the sound of flaming icy silence on the other end?

"We'll talk about it some other time," Robert said, and hung up.

She had a hard day before her to get through, an editorial conference, a late lunch with an irascible English historian who had threatened he might get better terms with Doubleday, a Monday pile of letters to be dealt with.

Scrub it all, go home and let the great wave she now saw in full clarity break over her head, take and overwhelm and drown her?

No. For some reason she was afraid, in heart and body, to go home. He might be there.

It wasn't a question of summoning the courage to call him back and say, "What on earth did you mean?"

There was no doubt whatever about what he had meant.

Perhaps as a kind of saving, cushioning force against accepting—from a cloudless sky—sudden and total disaster, at first fury took over. A cold and orderly fury. Let's see. He thought I knew he was having an affair with someone, unsuccessfully covering it up with his tales of long nights at work, too late finishing to come home and disturb me.

He might even sketch in for himself little secret telephone calls or whispered chats, on her part, with their friends. "Am I mistaken or could Robert possibly be . . . ?"

From where he sat, she had found it all out, all about (who *was* she? again, one of their friends?) and had chosen to inform him of her discovery with this cruel elaborate expensive joke, bed and bedding delivered to his door.

"When you must sleep away from me, sweet dreams, my darling Robert." What wit and style and calm, what pointed savagery those words must have conveyed.

After four years of marriage, that he would think her even remotely capable of this inhuman . . . lunatic . . . behavior was the scald that for an hour or two or three diverted her attention from the all-but-mortal pain of the wound beneath.

She got through, survived her day at Faunt and Faunt, until four-thirty and then left in the middle of dictating a letter—"I'll finish it tomorrow morning, Eve, I must rush off, people coming for dinner"—and took a taxi to the apartment.

No one to face, after all. Nothing to face, except, nothing. One of the suitcases gone from the top shelf of his closet, bureau drawers left, in haste, half open. Two or three suits gone. No note.

Only silence, soon ripped apart by the distressing noises of grief.

Robert's older brother Everett rang the doorbell at eight o'clock. Emily's eyes were so swollen with weeping that she could barely make out, through the peephole, who it was.

He looked at her when he came in and said, "Oh, Emily dear. Oh, hell." He put an arm around her and led her to her favorite corner of the sofa. "I'll get us both a drink. Have you eaten? I'll heat some soup or something while I'm about it."

His presence was more than welcome. For a few bad moments a while back, Emily had thought, What if I start screaming? All alone, screaming.

Coming back with two glasses full of ice cubes in one hand and a bottle of scotch in the other he said, "Robert called me from Los Angeles. If he were a woman, I'd say he was hysterical. As he's a man, I will put it this way—he was blown to pieces."

"That makes two of us," Emily said in a hoarse watery voice a little above a whisper.

Of course, Los Angeles. DeVries, the producers of "Cityscape," had its home offices there and Robert had to fly out on short notice three or four times a year.

Had he not, then, left her?

Just gone off on a business trip?

Had this happened at all?

Yes.

"I'm not apologizing for him," Everett said heavily. "But I don't know if he ever will, or can, explain." And then he told her about Vera Moore. Vere.

"It wasn't a matter of idle dallying, four years married, enough is enough, nothing like that at all, Emily," he said. His involvement with Vere, his tearingly unhappy love affair, had been going on for at least two years before he met and married Emily. Vere couldn't or wouldn't leave her husband, older than she was and in delicate health—which later turned out to be leukemia. "Also quite rich," Everett added, looking thoughtfully into his glass. Five months ago Walter Moore had died. Vere went to friends at Cap Ferrat to get herself back together again. And then had gone straight to New York, and to Robert, and had said something along the lines of, Darling, here at last I am.

"I wish to Christ it hadn't gotten to you," Everett said. "He—well, obviously—talked to me about it. I thought it might burn itself out . . . and the ashes would all blow away before you . . ."

She saw no point in telling him now that it hadn't gotten to her. No point in telling him about that ghastly bed.

"But it isn't out yet, the fire?" she asked politely.

"I don't think he knows where he is right now, he's so torn up with guilt, past and present all mixed up so that he can't find his footing . . ."

"And now, the situation being reversed, she wants him to divorce me?"

"I don't know . . . he hasn't said . . . things aren't that clear, at least to me and I suppose to him . . ." Everett, calmly handsome Everett, was sweating now, and openly wretched.

"Well, if he's in communication with you, tell him that on my part of course there will be no problem. Whatever." Hearing her voice, she amazed herself, disliked herself; but in some way was proud of herself.

"Now look, Emily—"

"I'm not awfully good at standing around waiting for passions to run their course—for fires to burn themselves out. And then, the flames might leap to the next rooftop, and the next."

"He's not like that. He never was and never will be like that."

"I don't, strangely enough, know what he's like," Emily said. "Not right now, anyway. Isn't that funny? By the way, do I smell soup or something scorching?"

She didn't go in to work the next day. If she could hardly recognize her face in the mirror, what would other people think about it?

Robert called her at twelve. "I talked to Everett last night after he left you. Did I really get your message straight? About divorce? Do you really, Emily, mean it?"

His voice was neither hard nor soft, but tightly controlled; it might be an illusion that under the voice was a suggestion of tears in the throat.

Did he expect her to get down on her knees,

retract, plead with him? Good old forgiving modest Emily. Let's give ourselves another chance, Robert. I'll just sit back and grit my teeth and wait until . . . Was he waiting in terror for this gentle, cowardly compromise?

"Yes, I really—Robert—meant it."

After a short pause, "I'm sorry. In every possible way, my sweet, my . . . constant nymph."

A thrush sang overhead. A breeze lifted Emily's hair. She put an uncertain hand to it. Did good manners, or just sheer silence-filling, call for an inquiry as to how Vere was? As far as she knew they had never married, but then lots of people didn't, anymore.

No. No inquiry about Vere. And no lingering here, where peace no longer sifted down from the trees and up from the crystal-green of the goldfish pool.

"I must, as a matter of fact, go find her— Flora."

"I'll walk you to her," Robert said.

"Please don't trouble." All right, go ahead and say it, why not? "In a setting like this I really prefer my own company."

"It's no trouble. And in a setting like this I prefer yours. You're looking amazingly—what?" The scarred eyebrow rose a little. "Amazingly Emily."

"Well then, not having a compass or map, I suppose the quickest way is the way I came." She moved swiftly past him, up the grassy slope, to follow the stream the other way, with him at her side after the first few steps.

The fast walking was a good excuse for still being a little wanting in breath. "And you—are you with people, or . . . ?"

"No, alone. Do I see someone beyond that trellis-work over to the left waving at you?"

Flora, thank God. "I hope you didn't miss the white wisteria," she called. "I was about to take the tiniest cutting but a gardener—I suppose he was a gardener, he had a trowel sticking out of his pocket—came along and—" She stopped and looked at Emily's companion with lively curiosity.

"This is Robert. Robert Marne—Flora Wallace."

"How do you do, Mr. . . . *oh.*"

She knew that Emily's former husband, and this must be he, had something to do with making movies, and had put together a sketchy mental picture of him, based on what she had read or heard of the world of films. An unnerving finger-snapping type, visibly under the influence of some exotic drug; certainly wearing a massive mustache and probably a beard as well. Hardly the sort of man you associated with Emily, but then certain people had a way of choosing odd mates.

The man she now met was tallish and thin with fair receding hair, thoughtful eyes (something curiously enticing about the scar-split eyebrow), long cheeks, and a sharply cleft chin. He looked as if he might be a professor of English literature at one of the better universities. His voice, acknowledging the introduction, was Bostonian. His clothes were good, and easily worn, a suit of greenish-olive tweed.

"Too bad about your cutting," he was saying. "Why didn't you just tell the man to go mulch himself? Shall we go back and try again?"

Flora found herself for some reason immediately charmed by Robert Marne. Really, she thought, this is most disloyal, after what he did to Emily. Perhaps, reassuringly, if and when she got to know him better she wouldn't like him at all.

"Thanks, but I think not. Stealing is bad enough in front of Emily." She thought Emily looked uncomfortable, and vulnerable, and strangely unlike herself. A splash of pink on each cheek, the eyes behind the tortoise-rimmed glasses not their usual soft harebell blue but brilliant, darker. Get her out of this? Whatever this was? "And we'd better be getting back to the car."

"Which way are you heading?" he asked.

"Well, we do wander more or less at will but . . ." Something about his eyes, a courteous but unmistakable demand in them, made her continue, "We're staying at the Carrack Arms near Chichester tonight."

"Oh, good. My destination too. Can you give me a lift there? My car is—oh, a long story, I won't bore you with it."

After a brief hesitation, "Yes, if you don't mind the front, with our driver. We're rather a

28

muddle of wraps and odds and ends, and a poodle, in back."

Several hours later, when she and Emily were visiting the bathroom in a little country pub where they also drank cold fresh lemonade, she said apologetically, "I'm sorry, Emily, but I didn't see how I could flatly refuse him to his face."

"Of course you couldn't," Emily said. "After all, he isn't a highwayman."

Flora thought she had devised a way to get them through the afternoon's drive without possible awkwardness and discomfort for Emily, having to converse with Robert.

As they left the parking lot at Brow Hall, she rummaged around her feet. She traveled with a number of containers: a large leather handbag, a crewel-embroidered shopping bag, and a British Airways tote, all jammed full. From the shopping bag she took a thick paperback, *The New Oxford Book of English Verse*.

"It is our custom in the afternoons," she announced, "to refresh ourselves with poetry. People seem to have so little time for poetry these days. I hope you won't mind listening too—may I call you Robert?"

"Certainly not," Robert said. "That is, I'd like to."

This custom came as a surprise to their driver; a method, obviously, for quenching conversation. He gave a quick curious look at the man on the seat beside him and found himself being studied as quickly, in return. Odd thing in a way; the man had come up to him in the parking lot while he was walking Leo and had said, "I'm to connect at some garden around this neighborhood with a woman named Denver, Emily Denver. I don't suppose you . . . ?"

After a moment, Denis decided to enlighten him. He looked perfectly all right. An American, must be a friend of hers meeting her by prearrangement.

"We are taking Mr. Marne to the Carrack Arms," Flora told Denis when the three had returned to the car.

"I believe your road lies through Mendham," Robert added. "If you'll stop a minute at the inn there I'll pick up my bag."

Settling herself and forcibly restraining Leo from jumping over the seat back to investigate and befriend this new passenger, Flora opened her paperback. "Spenser's *Epithalamion,* I think," she said. "It looks, yes, as though it will take us a good long way."

Emily, grateful, half listened and was able to devote herself to asking unanswerable questions in her head.

. . . "Now lay these sorrowful complaints aside;/And having all you heads with girland crownd,/Help me mine owne loves prayses to resound" . . .

Questions such as, was he joining his Vere at the Carrack Arms? Were they to make up a jolly party there—after all, three long years under the bridge?

How in the *hell* had he managed to turn up, in all of England, at Brow Hall?

She had explained to him what she was doing there, but he hadn't troubled to reply in kind.

Her office had a casual and tentative itinerary she had written the day before she left, in case they wanted to get in touch with her; but in these circumstances, a sheet of paper three thousand miles away didn't make any kind of sense.

Pure mad coincidence, she was forced to conclude. And strangely enough the kind of thing that happens all the time.

FOUR

The last Brixton visit Tickell had had from Luce was five months ago, although she still continued to send him joke cards every few weeks. "I don't particularly care for this place," Luce said of Brixton. Possibly because some time back one of her brothers had spent time there for stealing cars. He hoped and assumed she still lived in Call's Lane. He couldn't think why she would move. Her bleary old aunt owned the house and let her have the flat for a fraction of the going rate.

This was a help, because he still had his key, handed back to him with his clothes and odds and bits when he was released from prison. He spent his first few days as a free man with his sister in Liverpool. It wasn't affection that sent him there, but the fact that she owed him some money before he went in and had promised to pay him back when he got out.

The fuss was just about what he'd expected: she

was short of funds, she claimed, she'd have to look around and see if she could borrow the eighty-five pounds from someone, and so on and so forth. Tickell sat adamantly in her front parlor drinking bottles of her beer and at the end of the second day she coughed it up, counting out each note with thin reluctant fingers. ". . . and how I'll get through the rest of the month I'm sure I don't know, John." Tickell grinned at this and said, "You'll just have to dip into your ten or fifteen thousand or however much you've got squirreled away."

He thought it might be a useful idea to pay a first visit to the flat when Luce wasn't there, just to look things over and see in general how things were. To find out if she still worked at Gullion's, he telephoned there and asked to speak to her and was told to wait a sec, she was at the other end of the bar. Instead he hung up and made his way to Call's Lane.

The flat consisted of a large untidy but comfortable sitting room, a small bedroom, a long narrow bathroom, and a good-sized kitchen. As usual, the kitchen was a mess. Walking silently in case someone in the flat below was listening and wondering what Luce was doing at home at this hour, Tickell wandered about, hands in his pockets, eyes rakingly keen.

No sign of a man in residence here, but she might have done a hurried clear-out of any such evidence. In the bedroom, he got down on his hands and knees and peered under the bed. He made a long arm and pulled out a pair of socks, men's socks, which had collected puffballs of dust. Washed out, they'd do him nicely. He did this laundering task at the kitchen sink, hung the socks with the dish towels, and looked into the cupboard. Beer right at hand, six bottles of it. He opened one, rinsed out a glass sticky with orange juice, and sat down at the kitchen table.

As had always been her habit, she kept a careless jumble of bills, receipts, correspondence, and any pieces of paper she didn't know what else to do with, shoved between the sugar bowl and the salt shaker. Tickell picked up this sheaf and went through it. Behind in her bills, but that was Luce. One of her weird reminder lists, "geranium—call Maxie—hash." What kind of hash? To cook and eat, or consume in another fashion for another hunger? Tickell didn't believe in drugs himself. Too untidy, and a constant snatch-and-grab, wear-and-tear, on your own pocket. In between a gas bill and a card with a dentist's appointment written on it, he found a note which looked as though it had been crumpled up and then retrieved and smoothed out a little. "Luce, I'm off. I've very much enjoyed the spin with you. Luck in everything, and take care. Denis." He read this, and the post-script.

It was all he could do not to pick up his beer bottle and hurl it smashingly at the mirror between the windows. But, possible listeners upstairs and down, watch it. Save the luxury and relief of letting go for another, safer time and place.

He finished his beer and went on with his thoughtful prowl of the flat. She'd probably have put his clothes in the boxroom in the cellar; there was no sign of them in any closet. The boxroom key as always hung on a string next to the front door. He tinkered with the idea of going down and seeing what was in the boxroom besides his own things and thought no, that could wait till later, till they came home together, tonight. It was time to go and take a look at Luce herself.

If, one chance in fifty—no, a hundred—the police took it into their heads to watch what he did, at least for a little while after he got out, his behavior pattern would look disappointingly normal. Released man goes to visit sister in Liverpool, family ties and all that. Returning to London, goes to his once-upon-a-time girlfriend's flat, finds she's out, remembers she works as a barmaid at Gullion's pub in Kensington, or did last time he heard from or about her. Heads, naturally enough, for Gullion's.

(He had a pretty good idea who had informed on him but you didn't, under that possible police gaze, head straight to deal out punishment just out of nick. Maybe later. Nothing fatal, for the weasel Totten. Just highly unpleasant. And untraceable.)

In the bathroom, he washed his face and hands and combed his hair. He was a strongly built man of medium height. His hair had turned prematurely gray in his late twenties and because sometimes noticeable hair was a nuisance he was a collector of headgear. He didn't want to dye it because he was vain of the thick silvery shock, and enjoyed the fact that it confused people: "How old are you anyway?" He was thirty-six. He generally wore an amiable expression, which by some was considered misleading, and a structure of muscles made what seemed like a near-smile tilt up his lip corners. His clothes were fresh and on the conservative side, his short-trimmed nails always clean, his shoes always polished; none of your ratty-tatty look for him. He did not look at all dangerous.

He had a habit of humming to himself, sometimes not even aware he was doing it, which had driven one of the prison guards nearly crazy. The man in the next cell, who had had the benefit of a university education, informed him that it was a neurotic habit, a fear of silences. He hummed now, something he didn't know the title of, something about whenever spring breaks through again.

Gullion's was not a dressy pub, but large, old, comfortable, and just shabby enough to fit the cross-run of its patrons like a pair of slippers. There was a large room at the front, with the mahogany bar running the length of it to the right and leather chairs and built-in benches around the other three sides. At the rear was a second room devoted to the playing of billiards, the separating curtain made of long strings of rattling green beads. Lord Low often came to Gullion's, from his splendid house around the corner; and assorted teachers from Mrs. Conover's School on May Street; charwomen came there, and pretty girls and their men. Musicians for some reason favored Gullion's, and so did certain members of the London half-world, people who dipped their fingers into vaguely illegal matters.

The eighty-year-old twins, the Misses Mc-Guntrie, who drank their half pints every evening at Gullion's, thought there was something delightfully wicked about an occasional face. And something pleasingly masculine and perhaps a little wicked too about the playing of billiards amid clouds of blue smoke, bets openly placed on this shot and that unless there was a policeman refreshing himself at the bar.

Della McGuntrie paused in the act of lighting a Gaulois as the entrance door opened and a man in a dark green suit came in. "That," she whispered to her sister, Dolly, "is a man named Tickell, who must have been let out of prison."

Dolly's memory was not as good as Della's. She could recall every detail of her childhood, but she could not immediately bring to mind what they had had for dinner last night—was it baked beans on toast or asparagus on toast?

"Tickell," she said tentatively. "Did he—*kill* someone?"

"No, no. Lydia was on the jury." Lydia was their niece. "A robbery, four or five years ago. I believe a diamond necklace, and pearls, and valuable rings and silverware. They caught him almost immediately so"—Della was a devoted reader of detective fiction—"one suspects an informer. There was another man, an accomplice, or partner, or whatever the term would be. He was never caught. He got away with a great many valuable things too. It was thought at the time that he'd left the country. I remember his name, it's the sort of name that stays with you. Yore. Albert Yore."

"As in, days of yore?" Dolly asked.

"Exactly."

Unaware of their fascinated gaze from a dim corner, Tickell walked up the crowded length of the bar to the far end and said, "Hello, Luce."

Her back was to him as she reached for a bottle of whiskey on a high shelf behind the bar. She spun around. "Hello, Tick," she said.

She was a whip-slender girl in her mid-twenties, with a flat, snub-nosed, creamy face, pale flashing green eyes, and slippery satiny black hair which she wore in a dutch bob. She used her hair as another girl might use her hands, voice, or eyes. She spilled it softly at you or snapped it at you. She employed it for comment or complaint. For Tickell, she swung her head backward, the hair rising and flying in excited wings before it fell back again.

"Wait till I serve this and then we'll share a toast." After a few seconds, she pulled two pints of special bitter and across the bar they clinked mugs.

He'd almost forgotten how pretty her voice was, a lazy warble. "Hail the conquering and all that. Have you found a place to lay your head yet?"

"I think so. A nice little flat in Call's Lane. If you still live there, that is."

"I suppose," she said, with a grin, "I can tuck you in with the rest of my admirers. For the time being, anyway."

She wasn't a girl you ordered around, which was one of the things Tickell liked about her. He found himself glad that she was glad he was back—or at least seemed to be. "You're in luck, this is one of my early evenings."

He had no way of knowing that it was wounded vanity, or something more basic, painful, and hardly recognizable to Luce, that made her physical welcome to him a few hours later so spectacular.

At some time in the night, she woke briefly. She had been dreaming about Denis and now thought she heard his name or an echo of it. Had that been part of the dream or had she said it out loud? *Oh, Denis . . .*

Tickell at her side stirred and mumbled, "What . . . ?"

"Dreaming," Luce yawned back. "About—was it Ma Benson? She's the manageress at Gullion's, been there a year or so. Yes. Ma Benson. Crazy."

Tickell reached out a strong arm for her.

"Crazy is right. Dreaming about *women.*"

Falling comfortably into old habits, Tickell cooked breakfast, a nice fry-up of sausages and several slices of ham that looked a bit wan and shriveled but smelled all right, scrambled eggs and toast. After that they went down to the boxroom to investigate the condition of his wardrobe. There were no moth holes to worry about because most of his suits and pants and jackets were made of synthetics. In a large paper carton, there were ten or so shirts, socks and underpants, ties and belts. Another large carton held his hats. His shoes were dusty but intact, five pairs of them. A metal box held tiepins and miscellaneous small finery, including an expensive Swiss watch with an alligator strap he had stolen years ago.

"We'll bring everything upstairs, Luce, all right?" In this casual way he asked a large question.

Waking a second time before dawn, she had formed a shadowy plan about which she wasn't at all sure. Give it time.

"Yes, all right. You'll want some time to find work and after that we can look around and see where we are."

Occasionally in their long on-and-off association, when his daily work lay a good distance away from Southwark, he chose to live conveniently nearby the job, dropping around on weekends at Call's Lane if he wasn't involved with another girl at the moment. Or if, in turn, she would tell him to lay off for a couple of months, okay?

After he had found drawer and closet space for his things, Tickell poured them out a second cup of coffee and took a cigarette from the pack in his shirt pocket. He stared at the unlit cigarette.

"Where's my cigarette case? It wasn't in the lock-box."

"I used it for a while, sort of to remind me of you, and then I . . ."

"Then you what?"

She didn't like the look on his face at all. Every once in a blue moon, he was inclined to try it on, bullying her. Let him see right away there was to be none of that.

"I gave it to someone," she said coolly. "After all, it wasn't real gold, only gold-washed. But he thought it looked like Fred Astaire or something."

"Gave it to who?"

"I forget. Let me think—" indicating with a snap of her shining hair that a great many men had passed through her life while he was in Brixton. "His name was Denis." She liked the sound of the name on her lips. It seemed to bring him nearer, bring him here.

"I don't suppose he'll mind returning it to its rightful owner? Where can I find him?"

Carelessly, "I have no idea. He was a long time ago."

"Denis. Denis what?"

"Mmmm . . . some name that sounds like a

city. Manchester? Or was it Taunton?—probably.''

Tickell's mind circled about the man's given name. Those syllables she had uttered in the night. Leaving off the ''Ma,'' Benson and Denis could sound remarkably alike, especially in a dream-blurred voice.

''He was a long time ago.'' Then how about that crumpled note on the kitchen table? Would it still be there after months, years?

Luce still didn't like the look on his face. ''I can't see what the fuss is about. You didn't use the case that much. And it was all scratched up inside.''

He'd been in bed with a chill and a terrible headache, and had dosed himself with a tumblerful of brandy, when the police came for him. He had only a frantic few minutes to get dressed and ready. He was allowed to use the bathroom after the police had checked it and found it had no window. ''See you don't slash your wrists in there and make a mess,'' said one of the two men with a grin.

He had only been in prison once before, when he was nineteen, and he wasn't sure how it would affect him at this age. Affect the workings of his mind, that is. His eye fell on the cigarette case on the glass shelf under the medicine cabinet. He took his penknife from his pocket and hastily scratched his secret geography on the underside of the lid. Not that he'd probably need it, he'd never forget the place—or would he? His brain felt like a bundle of sodden feathers right now.

He put the case into the long flat metal box which held small objects of value, some purchased, some stolen. He locked the box and put it back in its usual hiding place from any casual Southwark thief, under and in back of a pile of sheets and towels in the linen cabinet.

Then he flushed the toilet, and went out to the waiting police.

FIVE

On their arrival at the Carrack Arms, there was a getting out of passports and signing of names on register cards. Emily out of the corner of her eye watched Robert's hand as he filled out his card. His name and no other: no Vera Marne, or Vera Moore, no Vere at all. Reminded of Gertrude Stein's observation about Oakland, California, "There is no *there* there," she mentally rephrased it, "There is no *Vere* here."

Joining him later, perhaps. None of her business in any case.

It was a great relief, after the confinement of the car, and the selections from *The New Oxford Book of English Verse* (dear kind Flora) to be alone in the silence of the big comfortable bedroom, its windows a restful flickering of late-day green-and-gold willows close against the inn wall. She took a deep lazy bath and, dressing, found herself studying herself with unaccountable attention.

She had often wondered why so many women named Emily looked like Emilys. Did you, inescapably, grow into this foreordained resemblance? To her mind, or imagination, an Emily was not a particularly noticeable type, had brown hair, often wore glasses, and was inclined to have something to do with books. A wren name, it seemed to her, her mind roving over the tall creamy Ursulas, the dashing Maggies and Lizes, the fragrant Rosemarys and stately dark Barbaras, the fair Helens and chic Pollys. And silvery slender Veres.

The black linen might look, to him, like some sort of halfhearted stab at glamour. She chose instead a lilac-pink shirtdress, pretty and fresh but under no circumstances to be considered seductive. She was brushing her hair, which was short, soft, and of a light-shining brown, when there was a knock at her door. Flora, probably, come to talk Robert over.

Robert, when she opened the door, said, "May I come in? Do you still like a martini before dinner?" He held a tray with a frosted pewter pitcher and two cocktail glasses on it, along with a little saucer of olives. He advanced firmly into the room and put the tray down on a table in front of a flowered chintz loveseat.

"*Epithalamion* and about eleven pages of John Donne, and the ancestry of an apricot poodle are all very well," he said, "but we haven't had time to exchange more than a word or so, you and I.

Come here and sit down, Emily.''

Put away the feel of the heart distressed and the knees a little shaky. Look upon this as the thing you handled as a matter of course at Faunt and Faunt—easy, amiable conversation over cocktails with a writer, even a difficult writer, even a total stranger.

She sat down beside him and lifted her glass. ''Oh, lovely. Thank you. Cheers. How have you been, Robert?''

He smiled faintly. ''I've been quite well. An up here, a down there.'' And, almost mocking her cool pleasant manners, ''How have you been, Emily?''

''Ditto, I'd say.'' Don't move to the personal. Don't say, You haven't told me what you were doing at Brow Hall. His non-explanation to Flora, ''My car is . . . I won't bore you with it,'' was familiar to her. When Robert didn't want to explain things, or embark upon long stories—he disliked on-and-on ramblings from anybody's lips—he resorted to, I won't bore you with it. Very convenient. On occasion she had adopted it herself.

But do say something clear, and hard (in two senses of that word). A long overdue obvious question. ''How is Vere?''

''Well too, I hope. I haven't seen her for a year. More properly, fifteen months.''

Emily could find nothing but an ''Oh?'' She took a sip of her martini, the best kind of Robert martini, dry and crisp but not spine-rattling.

Well, people did for various reasons blow apart. She and Robert had blown apart.

She thought that just for a moment or two, he looked older, and tired. And in some fleeting way, lonely.

More for his sake than hers, she said, "It's a long story and you won't bore me with it."

"Not now at any rate." He put down his drink, leaned to her, put an arm around her, and kissed her, very lightly and delicately, on the mouth. She thought he murmured, "Just checking," but wasn't sure.

There was another knock at the door. He got up and opened it to Flora, who was grasping together her paisley-printed dress at the small of her back.

"Oh dear, sorry—I was just going to ask Emily to do up all these maddening little buttons, in back, covered buttons, you see, with loops, so that . . . I suppose I could have put it on backward and buttoned it, but then, the sleeves—"

"I'll go down and get another glass and another pitcher while you button, Emily." And to Flora, "I think it's nicer in here than in the bar, don't you?" His eyes swept the room and in some way saw it intimately for all of them—the wide bed canopied in ivory linen, the soft blue of Emily's robe tossed across it, the late sun striking a rope of crystals Emily had not yet made up her mind whether to wear, slung over the bathroom doorknob.

When the door had closed behind him, Flora said a little enviously, "Nothing seems to faze these international people. Or, I suppose he is? He seems to know his way around. But if you were having a reunion, I'm sorry to have burst in on it."

"No reunion and no reason to be sorry," Emily said. "Just as you observed, man of the world coping with stumbling over an ex-wife beside a pool of goldfish."

"But I still don't see—I mean, just jumping into the car with us like that, and stopping to pick up his bag from where he was staying in Mendham. And the man at the desk here said he was lucky, they had a room even though he hadn't made a reservation."

Emily took a long and welcome swallow of her drink. "He's never been much given to what the *New Yorker* used to call The Department of Fuller Explanations."

As they went down the oak-banistered stairs to dinner, Robert said, "I reserved a table in the smaller dining room by the window, will that suit you?"

"Probably. We've never been here before, have you?" Flora was determined to extract some information from this mysterious man. For, she assured herself, Emily's sake. Get things in perspective for Emily. Human question marks were unnerving.

"No. I looked it over though, while you two

were dressing, or napping, or whatever you were up to."

Flora thought how (although in a rather exciting way) comfortable he was to be with. And he must have done some dressing, himself: fresh striped shirt, different tie, well-soaped skin tight down the long wittily seamed cheeks.

Their table by the window looked out into an arbor of honeysuckle and grapes pierced with the last few arrows of low sunlight. The window was open, the scents were soft, all was green, murmurous and romantic. The lighted candle centering the table made everyone look remarkably well. Even me, Flora decided, catching a glimpse of herself in a mirror on the oak-paneled wall.

"I suppose we all have room for one more drink?" as a plump rose and gold waitress appeared at his elbow. "Then a little wine to celebrate this . . . unexpected encounter."

"All I know about films is what I see on the screen," Flora said, buttering a roll to help sop up her new cocktail. "As it doesn't seem likely that you are on a garden tour too, are you working? Or playing? Or looking for undiscovered talent? Or—or lining up camera angles?"

"Actually, you've all but hit on it," Robert said with an air of flattering surprise. "I've got hold of a book, rather obscure but promising. The time is the so-called Golden Age before the First World War." The drinks now arriving, he raised his glass. "To—what should it be? Yes, to us."

"To us," Flora repeated a little doubtfully. "The three of us."

"The story is a sort of Lady Chatterley in reverse. A very rich and proper Englishwoman falls madly in love with her gardener. He is not only married, with children, but a devout Scottish Calvinist. He leaves her employment in righteous indignation after a scene in which she . . . well, I won't go into that."

It crossed Emily's mind that he might just be making this up as he went along, and for what obscure reason she had no idea. Teasing Flora? On the other hand, her own professional field at Faunt and Faunt was non-fiction and she could hardly consider herself a walking catalogue of every work of fiction ever published.

But it was unlike him to run on and on as he did; he had always considered the recounting of plots of books or movies a black social sin. "She pursues him, over a period of several years, from great house to great house, from job forcibly fled to the next job. Ever since *Brideshead,* you know, there's been a public thirst for grand English houses, castles, and so on, so that we get a panorama of . . ."

At the waitress's return, Emily interrupted firmly and hungrily. "The fresh asparagus soup, the grilled trout, no potatoes, and a tomato salad, please." The two others ordered and Robert implacably resumed.

". . . Finally he decides he must kill her, to maintain his own sanity and virtue. Oh, wait a minute, our wine." He lifted one finger and the waitress devotedly returned. "With your trout, Emily, and our beef, a rosé ought to do it. Bring us a large carafe of the house rosé, if you will." He turned to Flora. "Interesting, isn't it, the story? Which brings me to a question—where, by the way, are you going tomorrow?"

"Mulsey House," Flora said. "How does he kill her?"

"In a lily pool, under a fountain, late at night, and for a while it is thought she committed suicide, but then . . ."

"But there's a lily pool at Mulsey House," cried Flora, now thoroughly in the spirit of the thing. Emily quietly finished her drink. Yes, she thought, he must be making it up as he goes along. At least this part of it.

"So I seem to remember from somewhere in my notes. I might be able to arrange right away for shooting in August—these stately-homes people are often a bit hard-pressed and not unwilling to put up with actors and camera crews." He poured rosé, and as though struck in mid-pour by an entirely felicitous idea, said, "How would it be if I just came along with you? If I wouldn't be a nuisance?"

As everything seemed to be going so well and interestingly, Emily looking, as a matter of fact, charming and vividly at attention, Flora said, "Oh lovely, yes, do come. Old-fashioned of me, but it is nice to have an escort. Of course, Denis—but he doesn't like leaving the

51

Gaspard all by itself."

"Denis," Robert said musingly. "Speaking of undiscovered talent, he gives a slight impression of an actor manqué, as well as some other impressions I haven't sorted out. Where, by the way, does he lay his head at night? Does he sleep with you?—I mean, here at the inn?"

"He likes to find accommodations for himself, and after driving hours his time is his own. I do believe there's a touch of marjoram in this soup, as well as a bit of grated . . . is it lemon or lime? You'd know, Emily. Emily," she started to explain to Robert, "has an amazing detective's palate and—" Then she blushed. "But you'd know all about that. After all, you and she . . . In any case, delicious soup."

As the Carrack Arms objected to pets in guests' bedrooms, Leo by prearrangement was committed to the care of Denis for the night. In the perverse fashion of poodles, he was extremely fond of Flora, but his heart and soul had been given at once to Denis.

The Gaspard having been put away in a lockup garage, Denis strolled about and found a pleasantly modest pub named the Horsecollar which would be glad to oblige him with a room providing he didn't mind kitchen noises underneath it waking him up early.

"The dog and I are good sleepers," Denis said. The hours of motion in the car and the sound of the engine worked wonders with Leo's normally bubbling spirits.

As requested, he called Flora to tell her where the two of them would be for the night. He was half tempted to say he had found a nice Chinese opium-smoking parlor with a spare bunk where they could bed down; but only half tempted. Leo slept under his chair in the public bar of the Horsecollar while Denis drank several pints of bitter. He was just in the middle of a plate of good, hot shepherd's pie when he was summoned to the telephone. "Anyone here named Taunton, Denis Taunton? London call for Taunton," called the woman behind the bar. And when he got up from his chair, "You can take it in the hall where you can hear yourself and them."

It was Joe Kennan of Gold Star Car-Hire. Flora, in arranging her tour, had presented him with a rough plan of places she wanted to go but not necessarily in sequence. "I've called four bloody hotels," Kennan began indignantly. "Then I got Mrs. Wallace at the Carrack bloody Arms and she told me where I could reach you. There's a girl been round, bar girl from Gullion's, Lucetta Somebody. She says she has to get in touch with you. Life or death, she said. She put a strong case. I'm not saying I'd do this for everybody, but you're more or less top of my list, so here I am obliging."

In the four days since Denis had left her his goodbye note, Luce discovered that she wanted him badly, wanted him back, and to hell—as soon as it could be arranged—with Tickell.

She pursued for several days what she called her game of Twenty Questions, to find out where Denis might be. Finally, a man whose name she didn't know suggested that she try Kennan's.

Her faulty but not unnatural theory about his sudden departure was that, first, he had been upset about the quarrel, hurt, furious. And that, second, he had heard somewhere, probably at Gullion's, that Tickell was coming back from prison, Tickell, her sometimes man for the better part of ten years. Which would, of course, have made him even angrier. And hotly jealous: out with Taunton, in with Tickell. She couldn't imagine that he had fled because he was frightened of Tickell, finding them living together. She couldn't imagine Denis being frightened of anybody.

Frightened? Frightened. That just might do it.

Tidy up the quarrel, you idiot. Make it up with him right away, before things have a chance to cool off.

"She wants you to call her as soon as possible, meaning tonight, not at home but right away at Gullion's," Kennan said. "And some silly business about saying on the phone to whoever answers that your name is Brown in case they'd shout Taunton all over the place. Okay? Clear?"

"Yes. Thanks." Leo had gone to sleep on Denis's foot during the conversation. They went back into the bar and Denis finished his cooling shepherd's pie and bought another pint to sit and think with.

As far as he was concerned, there were no dangling emotional strings. Luce was quite simply over. But, life or death? What the hell was she up to?

Very much against his will, he called Gullion's and asked for her, in his annoyance giving his own name. "Brown," for God's sake.

She came on after about forty seconds. "I'm borrowing Ma Benson's snug, I didn't want to talk where people could hear. I'm scared silly, Den, I've got to get some help from you."

"Scared of what?"

"Tickell's out, but you must have heard about that, which is why I guess you— Anyway, someone told him about me and you and he's wild. He had to go off to Liverpool to get some money his sister owed him, but when he comes back I'm afraid he'll do something awful . . . with a broken bottle, or a knife. He has this frightful temper, one minute smiling and the next—"

"That's simple," Denis said. "Go to your beauty-shop friend's and stay with her for a bit. Or your aunt in Leicester."

"He knows these people. He'd know where to hunt for me. Don't you understand? I need *you*. After all, it's because of you, or me and you, that . . ."

"I'm on a driving job," Denis said, with forced patience. "Which puts me out of business as far as your worries are concerned. Three pieces of

55

advice. Go to the police and have them warn him off. Or get lost for a week or so, say Brighton or wherever you fancy. Or get a broken bottle of your own and sit it out. I've got to go, Luce, my passengers are breathing down my neck. Good luck.'' He hung up.

Luce sat in Ma Benson's snug considering, and then called Kennan's Car-Hire. Into her warbling voice she introduced a note of panic and a threat of tears. ''I was just on the line with Denis and we were cut off, right in the middle, just a click and a buzz—can you give me the number he was calling from?''

Kennan gave it to her.

SIX

Dinner and coffee over, they left the dining room and went into the pleasant candlelit lobby with its deep chairs, a well-trodden valuable-looking Kirman on the planked oak floors, and a pair of vases filled with burningly blue and purple delphiniums on a console table.

Robert gave every appearance of one at the center, rather than at the conclusion, of a happily companionable evening.

"Shall we sit down and have a brandy here or stroll out and find a pub?"

Flora declined. "I must catch up with my flower notes—there's a little corner at Brow I'd like to copy at home. The coolest mauve and blue columbines, or perhaps," to Robert, "you call them aquilegia. And behind them a river of nasturtiums pouring down the gray stone wall, a perfect blaze. Was there or wasn't there a young very dark cypress to set them off?"

Emily declined. "I have a book that is calling out very loudly to me."

"Oh. Well then, when do we leave here tomorrow?"

"Somewhere around ten," Flora informed him. "Time for lazy breakfast in bed. Thank you again for dinner." Robert had picked up the check, raising a calm dismissing palm to objections. "Don't forget you're doing me an enormous favor." After a glance at Emily, he added, "Providing me with vintage transportation— lovely car."

Having been forced, in her view, to retreat to her room, and don't trouble to ask right now why this retreat was necessary, Emily found herself indignant and restless. The book she said had been calling her fell silent under her uninterested eyes.

She felt not only wide awake but strung on wire. It was only nine o'clock and the possibility of a sleepless night stared her whitely in the face. In this latitude, in June, the evenings died very slowly into night. Outside her window the color was a clear deep lavender. Something fresh and sweet came in on the air, and looking out she saw that the arbor of honeysuckle and grape was underneath her window. A bird sang a little pierce of music, a thrush, she thought. It was too early, too beckoning, for thrushes to go to bed too. Or either.

She thought a brisk walk would be helpful, would make bed and book more tempting.

Walking alone here at this hour wouldn't seem silly and dangerous. Not in the English countryside, after the blossomy green day; not, being immersed as she was, in the feeling of physical safety that seemed to hover over the Carrack Arms. She pulled on a white cardigan and went out with her senses wide open.

A right turn along the road in front of the inn took her past a row of modest little houses, no display of money and no pretentions to style; but every front garden was deep in lavish bloom, the colors only suggesting themselves in the lavender light. She smelled roses, and stock, and unidentifiable scents, a mixture that went to the head. She felt unsettled, unreal, and under a spell of some kind.

A boy on a bicycle went by and waved a hand at her, otherwise she seemed to have the twilit road to herself. Everybody no doubt glued to the television screen. From an open door, a commercial floated, ". . . the batter is the better for the butter that's in it."

There was a soft crying meow from behind her and a large handsome Siamese cat moved to brush its creamy fur against her ankle. She bent to stroke its head and then decided it wouldn't do to loaf along like this if the purpose of her walk was to tire herself out. Pick up your feet, Emily.

The Siamese picked up his feet too, staying faithfully at her side, and she began to worry about him, straying too far from wherever he lived, getting lost. But then cats made their way across whole states, didn't they, seeking the homes from which for one reason or another they had been removed? Perhaps, though, the elegant Siamese breed never had had to develop this long-distance art because people as a rule didn't want to part with their beautiful Asians.

She stopped and looked severely down at the cat. "Go home!" she ordered, and had to suppress a smile. Ridiculous, thinking you could issue commands to cats.

From depths of darkness under a great willow a little ahead of her, she heard a breath of the laughter she hadn't allowed herself, then Robert's voice asked, "Do I hear Emily?" And, "Did you bring your book along?"

He emerged from the shadows of the willow. She saw that it was at the corner of a lane. He must have been coming down that lane, at right angles to the road, so surely he couldn't have been following her?

"I decided I needed some air." In both ways now: the thwack of surprise, unreadiness, playing tricks with her breathing apparatus.

"My idea too. Shall we go back up the lane? There's a pond, no goldfish to be seen unfortunately, but with a nice grassy bank to sit on. Don't worry about the cat. He's probably roaming around looking for love."

"If it's the long way back I don't think that I—"

"If anything it's shorter." He took her hand in persuasion; a very firm kind of persuasion.

"Come along, Emily, do."

After a second or two she took her hand lightly back and resisted the temptation to shove it into her pocket. It was deeper twilight in the lane, under the flanking murmuring willows. They walked fast, as they always had, together. "Most women just loll along," he had said on their very first walk, from the Metropolitan Museum down Fifth Avenue to the Minetta Tavern in the Village. "You really know how to get the use out of your legs."

The silence wasn't comfortable. "Do you like Flora, what you've seen of her? We're good friends, so be careful how you answer."

"Very much. Here's our pond coming up, right around this bend. Let's sit down in the grass and you can tell me all about Flora."

How many times today were civilized manners going to have to try to overcome her own wishes and needs? She didn't want this, any of this. She wanted instead, desperately, to get away, by herself, to get back to herself—whoever she was.

Damn you, Robert. And I was having such a lovely time, in a lovely vacuum holding nothing but gentle pleasures.

When they sat down in the long silky grass, he lit a cigarette and handed it to her. "You always liked a puff or two after you gave them up, do you still?"

"No thanks," but she took the cigarette. "I mean, yes." Delicious diversion, brief snatched relief. Hardly aware of it, she smoked for a moment or two and then tossed the cigarette into the water. Silence again.

"What was the name of that book you were so generously sharing the plot of, at dinner?" Malicious of me, she thought immediately. He gave her a look which she read as startled. He pulled a long piece of grass and nibbled at the stem. "As you wouldn't have brandy, I must content myself with chlorophyll. Oh, the book. *The Life and Death of Mrs. Blessingham.*"

"I must look it up."

Abruptly, he changed the subject. "I've heard —I forget who told me—that you're thinking of marrying again?"

"Yes."

"Anyone I, that is, we, knew?"

"No."

He put an arm lightly about her shoulder. The palm curved and pressed in strongly on her flesh and bone. His eyes were very close.

"Then we haven't much time, have we, Emily?"

Good-bye, good manners. She shook herself rudely loose of the arm, the pressing and caressing hand.

"What on earth do you mean by that?" she asked angrily, looking not at him but straight ahead of her.

"Just what I said." His voice was mild. "We haven't much time to be together—by odd coincidence—as we are now. And in this light, or lack of it, you can't see three dropped years very clearly. It's as though—"

"Is that from one of your scripts?" Say anything, however flatfooted, to stop him. "I must get back, Robert." She rose to her feet. "I'll leave you to your reminiscences."

He paid no attention to this dismissal but got up too. "I see we've lost the cat along the way," he said. "And as Flora put it, it's nice to have an escort, particularly in this dangerous darkling night. You might be attacked by a skylark, or something."

In seven minutes, in silence, they were back at the Carrack Arms. "Enjoy your book," he said in parting at the foot of the stairs. "And I will enjoy my brandy. And my reminiscences."

Take a long bath, read until your eyelids fall, and don't hash over nonsense murmured in the dusk, Emily ordered herself.

Was it just that the male ego wouldn't let a lost, an abandoned love, go? That she must still find him, as long as he was near, dear?

Do *not* hash things over.

Unconsciously, she touched the shoulder his hand had cupped. Then in a mirror she caught a glimpse of the hovering, remembering fingers and dropped her arm to her side.

She obeyed her own orders to the letter and shortly after midnight switched off the bedside lamp. The type on the pages of her book had begun to dance and crisscross in a promising way.

At some time between three and four o'clock

she snapped wide awake and her mind, her emotions, and her memories went on the boil.

"Come along, Emily, do." His voice, his burr-edged musical voice, seemed to resonate from the crown of her head down to her toes. The thin white line of the scar through his eyebrow—she had forgotten how it had always looked to her a bit raffish and at the same time strangely endearing. His eyes, and the modeling of his mouth suggesting both wit and will, the smell of him, salty sea-grass—

Oh God. He was in the room with her, he filled it, he was in her bed, turning to take her in his arms.

When it came to matters of major importance, Emily had over the years developed a habit of being, or trying to be, nakedly honest with herself.

It struck her now with desolating force and clarity that she still loved him. With, yes, all her heart.

It was as though with one careless stroke of his hand he had brushed away her whole future. All over again.

Or so it seemed at this dark hour.

Denis began to yawn over his paperback a little after midnight. The bed had proved not fit to read in, with its lank old pillow and the brass rods of its headboard vigorously attacking shoulders and spine. He sat in an armchair, considering a bottle of beer before sleep. Yes, why not. He opened it and reached for his gold-washed cigarette case.

He found himself, for the fourth or fifth time, studying with mild interest the scratches incised on the underside of the lid. A diagram of some sort which might or might not be a map. Four lines, two curved and two straight, and just to the right of where they converged a tiny circle with what looked to be an arrow or a V pointing at it. Under each of the four converging lines was scratched a letter: an O, and E; an X and a G.

This hieroglyphic might be Tickell's work; or perhaps he had bought the marked case secondhand or been given it by someone, just as Luce had given it, in turn, to him.

(He had spotted it in a desk drawer a few weeks after moving in with Luce, and immediately he started to whistle "Top Hat, White Tie and Tails." To Luce's amused raised eyebrows, he explained, "I'm a Fred Astaire buff." "Well, if it makes you want to whistle you can have it," Luce said. "It belongs to Tick, but he'll never miss it.")

Denis had so far only one identity for Tickell: a man sent to prison for helping himself to somebody else's jewelry and valuables. Was this by any chance a sketch map of the place to be robbed? Drowsing over his beer, he thought he might in an idle moment look up where it had happened, the robbery.

If he were, as he occasionally was, hard-pressed for cash, the scratches might turn Tickell's cigarette case into a very unusual and salable form of collector's item.

SEVEN ✤ ✤ ✤

Tickell told himself that the rambling and semi-circuitous route he chose to take to the village of Spill was a caution probably not at all necessary. Nevertheless, it felt better to him to do it that way. A bus to Benbury, where he changed to a slow train which after the morning commuter express runs turned itself into a local. An endless wait of an hour and a half on a platform under a bridge, his only fellow-traveler an elderly woman sitting on a bench beside a cage which held her elderly parrot. His utterances were limited to an occasional complaining croak, an indignant whistling, and on and off the summons, "Come along, George."

Come along is right, for Christ's sake, thought Tickell, gazing impatiently down the tracks as if jumping nerves could make the train arrive any minute now. Why was the woman staring at him? Probably because in this Godforsaken green tree-whispering place there was nothing else to stare at.

But in an odd way the waiting was a welcome vacuum. What if he got there and found . . . ?

For the thousandth time, he visualized a new housing estate, acres and acres of little houses with little lawns and little new trees. Or perhaps a manufacturing plant, miles of chain link fence around it. Or any number of other relentless marches of progress, in the course of which the towering trees would have come crashing down, the old stone walls rubbled away, the coarse grass and brambles ploughed under. And an old well with a rotting wooden cover would have been filled in. Of course—filled in. Who in the usual speedy corner-cutting rearrangement of the landscape would bother to excavate an old well? Landfill would pour into it, choke it, level it. There would be no hint except in villagers' memories that there had ever been a well there at all.

He hadn't dared to inquire of any of his visitors at Brixton, *Is there anything going on at Spill?* In the way of building, developing, new construction, that is.

If anything more immediately dramatic had been going on at Spill, surely it would have rated a paragraph, indeed a good deal more than a paragraph, in the newspapers, to which he had given attention every day of the four and a half years in Brixton. "Astonishing Discovery in Old Well at Small Somerset Village."

As if in reply to the parrot's final "Come

67

along, George," the two-carriage train ambled alongside the platform and stopped. Settling down by a dusty window, Tickell gave a quick wary glance at the other passengers. No one he knew, but why should there be? He felt at a moon's remove from London.

Nobody who looked like police.

Getting out at the Spill station, he looked about him uncertainly. He hadn't, that long-ago time, approached the town by rail but by road. He saw a pub across the street and felt a powerful urge for a drink. His throat was dry, and then there was the possibility of the housing estate or the manufacturing plant to brace up for.

But, as it had happened in this quiet little place, someone in the pub might recognize him. True, he had provided himself with heavily dark-rimmed glasses and a deep-brimmed tweedy hat which covered his hair except for a few strokes of gray at the sides. Still . . .

But if he was by any chance recognized, would it matter? He had been caught and sent to prison, and now he was free and that was that.

Well, chum, an imaginary voice in the pub said, and what are you doing returning to the scene of the crime? No—erase the word "crime." What are you doing back here where you had a go at burglary?

He couldn't openly lay claim to any acquaintance in the town, someone whom he had dropped by to visit.

It was Kemp, the Gadneys' gardener, who had set the whole thing in motion.

Tickell unconsciously turned his head to the right, but of course the Gadney place couldn't be seen from here, it must be at least a half mile away. The tremendous, show-off white-brick house with its foreign-looking slanting slate roofs and acres of privileged greenery and gardens, woodland edging a nine-hole golf course. And Mrs. Gadney's mother's fancy brick cottage at the far end of the drive, where it came out on Gulliver Road.

Did Kemp still live here? Or had the Gadneys fired him after the robbery, on the grounds that the police must have spent a good deal of time questioning him? Tickell had no idea.

Arthur Kemp, a bachelor, balanced his hard-working outdoor life with an occasional weekend blast in London during which he devoted his attention to drink and girls on an impartial basis: plenty of both. His girls were usually prostitutes, casually met, used, and forgotten. One of them, who had been treated to a long night's drinking before getting on with her regular occupation, was a sister of Albert Yore.

Several days later she said to Yore, with a wink, that it was too bad he didn't know of any light-fingered fellow interested in a good haul. Having secured his close attention, she told him about Kemp's disclosures over his fifth and sixth whiskies.

These people Kemp worked for in a town

named Spill, in Somerset—filthy rich and liked to let everybody know it. Mrs. G. didn't care to bother tootling off to a bank vault every time she wanted to put on her necklaces or rings or pins or earrings. These, and lord knows what other good things, were kept in a safe at the Gadney house.

Kemp, deadheading roses during an outdoor cocktail party, had heard, from the other side of the tall floribunda hedge, the combination of the safe. Mrs. G., the sunlight upon whose martini glass sent a crystal ray through the leaves into Kemp's eye, was urging a safe on her female companion. ". . . and I'll lend you my idea for the combination—do admit it's pure genius! My own name spelled forward and then backward." Mrs. Gadney's given name was Imogene.

As if that weren't enough, there was Mrs. G.'s mother, painted-up old bag as Kemp described her, who chose to live in the guest cottage because she couldn't stand Mr. G. Wouldn't use his safe, either, having stated that in some financial pinch he might be tempted to steal and sell her things. A child of the Dole, she had never found herself able to trust banks and kept her goodies in her baby grand piano. "Mean old bitch, hoards stuff, I wouldn't wonder," Kemp had added.

A week later, Kemp was surprised and flattered by a telephone call from London. Betsy Yore . . . now which one had she been? Oh yes, the blonde with wild petal-curly hair like one of his best chrysanthemums. He'd been such fun, she said, that she was inviting him as a special guest to her birthday party next weekend.

It was a small party. Yore was there, introduced as Tom Exham. Tickell was there, Dickie Brown for tonight. Kemp was the third guest. "Three gents, what a treat," Betsy said, and tossed her head in Kemp's direction with a dimpling smile. "But thank God I don't have to take you all on. Last come first served." Which started Kemp's evening for him with a fine glow.

An unlimited flow of drink began. On the rainy November night, Betsy's little flat on Titham Street was snug, there was an electric fire in the grate, voices and cigarette smoke filled the air. Later, Kemp's memories of the long, long evening were a little confused. At some point the two men had asked him where he worked, and Betsy had said, "Oh, tell them your marvelous crazy Gadney stories, Artie." After several more drinks the name of a man, Chirico, a friend of a friend of Yore's, appeared in the course of the conversation. And then . . . raggle-taggle, bit by bit coming back to him days, weeks later, but some of it lost forever . . .

If Kemp would, through Betsy, tip the nod as to when the Gadney house might be empty, at night, for a few hours . . . Chirico would pay a little visit and then do a generous split with Kemp . . . after all, these rich bastards, why not? . . .

Very drunk, proud of himself as the center of attention, vicariously a member of the filthy-rich set, Kemp filled their cup to the brim. The

Gadneys were members of a perishing little-theater group, and next Tuesday night a new production was opening, Mrs. Gadney in it and her crazy old bitch of a mother too. Mr. Gadney was the director. The maid and the cook would go to the show, they always did, otherwise there was hell to pay. As he, Kemp, didn't live in, he could always slither out of it, saying he had to visit his sick aunt or tend to a friend's foaling horse or some such. The play wouldn't start until eight-thirty, but they always left the house well before eight to dress and put on their bloody makeup and so on.

But how, he now wanted blurrily to know, was he to get his share, if . . .

No problem, he was assured. Chirico would get in touch with him by phone. Too dangerous to arrange a meeting and be seen together. *If,* that is, Chirico was interested, and wasn't on to something else in some other part of England or anywhere . . . he was expected back from Italy tomorrow sometime . . .

And then the talk turned to football, during and after which Kemp's memory blanked out completely.

In his early days in prison, Tickell had often thought with sour amusement of Kemp's no doubt frustrated rage. He could hardly complain to the police that he'd been done out of his rightful cut. And who the hell was this captured Gadney thief anyway? He wasn't named Chirico, he wasn't Tom Exham or Dickie Brown. A man named Tickell—not a double cross but a triple cross. The only picture of Tickell which had appeared in the newspapers at the time was of him with an open hand shielding his face from photographers.

The police thought all along that it had been at least partly an inside job, that someone at the Gadneys' place had provided a bundle of helpful information. But for all their hard patient work they couldn't put any kind of solid case of this nature together. All they got were clear-eyed virtuous denials from the gardener Kemp ("Tickell? Yore? For God's sake, until I read the papers I never even heard their names before."). In this statement he was convincing because he was speaking the entire truth. The same from the cook; the same, with floods of hysterics, from the maid.

Firmly preserving thieves' honor, Tickell maintained that he and Yore had overheard details, two men talking, in a pub in Houghcliffe, ten miles from Spill, and had based their plans on these drunken mutterings. He had been asked to describe the two men, and did; but they were never located.

As he was walking down the wooden steps from the platform, a girl in jeans on her way up stopped and said, "I don't suppose you'd know when the next train connecting with London comes in?"

He wondered if she had invented the question

so as to take a closer look at him. And hear his voice. He said, "No, I don't," and went rapidly down the last six steps. He didn't dare turn his head to see if she was still standing there gazing after him.

The little encounter made up his mind. Skip the longed-for pint or two. Walk as though with purpose, even if he hadn't yet gotten his bearings.

After all, it had been deep night when he had last roved Spill, in the car, and he had been in a panic, hardly able to think at all, much less register landmarks. He closed his eyes for a second to see mentally the scratches under the lid of his cigarette case. An X to indicate one of the road names . . .

There were road markers on the post on the next corner. By some marvelous impossibility, the one pointing north said Xavier Road. After a few cottages and a dairy farm, Xavier Road swung its gently shady curve through green fields and quiet woods. The walk couldn't, he thought, be much more than a mile. Even if he'd had a license, he wouldn't have wanted to go through the business of hiring a car, his name and identification, the date, papers to sign, mileage later totted up. The mere hiring of a bicycle from the stand at the bottom of the station steps would mean things written down on paper, even if he gave a false name. Which could, one chance in five hundred, show up upon later investigation of the reason for John Tickell's visit to Spill. Why, officialdom would muse, the fake name?

The farther along Xavier Road he got, the greater the tension mounting in him. In a way he wished he would find the housing estate, a bustle of cars, kids in prams, and the old scene vanished, wiped out forever. Nothing to hope for, but nothing to fear.

But everything, as in a dream, was exactly the same.

Here was the crossroads, where Xavier met Orme, Enderton, and Gulliver roads. Too obscure for commerce of any kind; no shops, one car going away in the distance, on Gulliver. Just the birds to be heard, and the breeze in the oaks and sycamores.

About a hundred yards up Orme from the crossroads, a memory of what had been a driveway made an opening in the moss-grown dry stone walls. He went along it, an old bent grove of willows on one side, immense oaks on the other. Now unseen from the road, he came upon the burned-out memory of a house, only the foundations left. Not a grand house but a small one, a cottage it must have been, with a blackened lean-to the only bit of it left standing.

A little, overgrown slope went down to the willows. A few tall pink and tangerine lilies remembered where there had once been a garden. Beyond the lost garden was a stone wellhead, of which the sheltering angled roof had also burned away.

Brambles caught at his trouser legs. Very near, he heard a sound eerily between a buzz and a whir and he stopped, his heartbeats crashing. A police listening device, newly installed and prepared to wait patiently for this secret visitor? Then his eye discovered the source of the sound: a small bird in a blur of wings poking its needle beak into a pink lily.

He walked to the well and lifted the cover by a rusted knob which had the remains of a heavy latch dangling from it, probably to keep forgotten children from investigating and tumbling in. A large amber and yellow butterfly landed floatingly on the stone rim. Its quivering-alive innocent beauty somehow enraged Tickell. He swiped it away with the back of his left hand.

An ancient silence came up to him from the well. Impossible to see the bottom, just impenetrable darkness there. He looked around for something to drop in and found half a crumbling brick a few feet away. He picked it up and then opened his fingers. Not a clatter, but a faint splash, far down. The well was not, then, dry. How deep did they build wells in this part of the country? There was, eventually—soon—only one way to find out.

He replaced the cover and stood making rough measurements with his eyes. How many feet of rope would be needed, to stretch from the waist of the oak on the far side of the drive, over to here, and down and down? He formed an idea of the length and thought he'd add another twenty feet just in case. How would you carry the rope? In a suitcase. Or maybe a backpack, with the proper clothing to go with it. Backpackers were an anonymous lot, just part of the landscape.

But there was something to be taken care of before that. Retrieve the cigarette case whose directional lines had guided him so accurately. Probably they'd make no sense whatever to anyone else.

But probablys were not allowable in a matter like this. Not even the shadow, the whisper, of a probably.

Denis. Denis who? Denis Taunton. Denis where? Find out, and fast.

He took an alternate route back to London, as interminable as the morning's, by train and bus, but the casual wandering look of his travels seemed now doubly important. In Rumpleford, finding himself exhausted, thirsty, and very hungry, he went to a down-at-the-heels workingman's pub, the Sword and Angel, and spent a long time over his mutton stew and his bitter.

Most of Luce's men, he recalled, had been first met at Gullion's, her social as well as her working world. Somebody at Gullion's ought to know something about a man named Denis Taunton. How recently he had been in London. And where he was now. And what he looked like.

A thorough grilling of Luce herself was out. She had already said she had no idea where Denis was. She had already said, "I don't see what all the fuss is about." Her first and obvious question would be, And why the hell do you want to find him anyway?

"What is it you want with him?" Jonesy asked a little blurrily at ten minutes to eleven in Gullion's pub.

Tickell had got there at seven-thirty and missed Luce by fifteen minutes. "One of her early evenings," Ma Benson replied to his inquiry. Tickell prepared himself for a long investigative evening.

In this atmosphere, a man could fall into easy chat with another man alone, or two other men; the bar was a species of easy-going club. A few there knew that Tickell was fresh out of prison and this gave a little extra interest to conversational exchanges. Nobody was tactless enough to mention his incarceration, but Tickell had no hesitation about opening gambits such as, "I've been away from this place for years, what's been going on around here? What ever happened to the dwarf who used to come in peddling camellias?" And, "Denis expected in tonight a bit later?"

Jonesy, working on his fifth pint, sounded promising because his question, "What is it you want with him?" had a suspicious, personal tone to it.

"He left a pile of his stuff at my girl's place and I thought I'd give him a chance to pick it up."

He looked, Jonesy thought, as if butter

wouldn't melt in his mouth, friendly, unruffled. "My girl" of course being Luce.

"I don't know—I haven't seen him for three or four days. He must be off on a job somewhere." Watch it; Tickell was Tickell. Jonesy was fond of Denis and now a helpful recollection came to him. "He said Kennan down the street—the Gold Star Car-Hire place—wanted him to go out on a driving job. For, did he say three weeks or so? I guess he took it. He didn't seem too wild about the idea. But these days you can't turn up your nose at a job. Especially an easy job like that."

"Oh well then, we'll just shovel his stuff into the boxroom."

In the closing-time bustle at eleven, he went to the phone, flipped through the directory, and called Gold Star. No answer, closed. Tomorrow morning, then.

When he got to Luce's flat, its emptiness sent its message as soon as he opened the door. Still out. Who with? Denis? Then he saw the note propped against the clock.

"Gone to Jessie's for a few days and a change. See you, Luce." It could have been deliberately mysterious, he thought, or then again just Luce's casual ways, coming and going exactly as she pleased, not a girl to be ready and waiting and taken for granted. He went to her closet and saw her only suitcase was gone from the top shelf. And along with it perhaps a third of the things on hangers.

For some reason he was, fleetingly, back in bed

beside her, waking up, hearing, he was surer and surer now, *"Oh, Denis."* And she thinking she could fob him off with dreaming about Ma Benson.

There was a certain comfort in the suspicion, even though it might be completely unfounded. It would provide a nice cover when and if needed.

"I'm looking for my girl Luce, who ran off for a bit of a fling."

He slept uneasily, and at eight o'clock made his way to Gold Star. When pursuing any important inquiry, his general rule was: If a side door is open, don't bother with the front door.

Just inside the open gate a tow-haired boy of seventeen or so was languidly sponging a black Toyota, a pail of soapy water beside him. Tickell stopped and said, "I wonder if you could help me out." He took a five-pound note from his wallet and both of them looked thoughtfully at it.

"I'm trying to get in touch with a chap named Denis Taunton. Can you find out for me if he's driving for you, and if he is, a general idea of the route? This is strictly between the two of us because"—winking broadly—"there happens to be a lady involved."

"Glad to, hold on for a sec," the boy said, and headed for the garage building at the rear of the yard. He was back in a few minutes. "Yes, he is. Driving for us, Taunton, I mean. Left Tuesday, two ladies, the one who paid the deposit was named Wallace. He took the Gaspard."

The boy's eyes lit up. "My God, that car. What

80

I'd give to drive her. Seventeen coats of paint on her, extra wire-wheel tire on the left front wing. A color you don't see on these tin cans"—sweeping a contemptuous arm inclusively over the rows of cars in the yard—"plum, with a cream top, canvas, a heavy kind they don't make anymore. And the butterfly grille—God!—sterling silver—"

"Yes, fine," Tickell interrupted with every appearance of impatience (nice to know exactly what the car looked like). "What's the route?"

"Pretty well all over the country. They're looking at gardens. Last night they stopped in Pym. Taunton put up at the Horsecollar there."

The five-pound note changed hands. The boy saw no reason for adding the information that he had had, after all, to consult Joe Kennan about the route.

"Who wants to know?" Kennan asked.

"Friend of his who stopped by."

Kennan gave him the route information and then said—incomprehensibly to the boy and with heavy sarcasm, "And I suppose this is another matter, second-go-round, of life and death?"

EIGHT ❧ ❧ ❧

Flora didn't after all have her breakfast in bed. Waking early and about to turn over for what she called another little snack of sleep, she remembered, yesterday afternoon on a narrow curving street approaching the inn, a particularly delightful shrub beyond a low honey-colored stone wall. The shrub, of a variety she had never seen or heard of, floated generously over the wall and cast its soft shadows on the brick sidewalk. Through the open car window the scent, as they passed, caught her like a whiff of paradise. The plumed flowers were a dramatic deep purple, centered with ashy blue.

She had found through long experience that on the whole it was better just to help yourself to cuttings or seed pods than apply to the owner for permission. In contrast to enthusiastic donors there were people who resented invasions of their garden privacies; or who tended to think you might mutilate their plants; or that even worse you might be prowling about on this odd pretext in order to set up a future robbery of the house.

Faint heart, she told herself, never won fair shrub. She pressed a button by the bed which said "Early tea," then dressed in what she considered unnoticeable garments suitable for a thief. The finishing touch would be a hooded brown raincape of balloon cloth. You never knew in England when it was going to rain, and the hood would conceal her hair nicely.

It was about a quarter of seven, after she had drunk her delicious tea, when she left the Carrack Arms, carrying her straw basket inside her crewelwork shopping bag. The sky was soft and gray. Yes, rain might indeed be impending. This would not in any way interfere with their plans for the day; she found a special pleasure in gardens in the rain, the quivering and glistening all about, the water-weighted bendings and released sweetnesses soaking the air.

If she was successful in her immediate expedition, she could mail the cuttings today (along with the pilfered dianthus from Sissinghurst Castle and the clematis "William Kennett" from Smallhythe Place) to her friends, the Dinnotsons, in Yorkshire. They had a large greenhouse and, amazing in this day and age, three gardeners. After the cuttings had established themselves and had gotten down to their work, Anne Dinnotson would send either the seeds or the roots, depending on the plant, to the

Wallaces' summer home in the Poconos, which was also equipped with greenhouse and gardener.

Yes, there was her bush, waiting for her around the curve in the road. Oh dear. The house, a small low house of stone, was only about fifteen yards from the wall. But the flowering green branches ought to protect her pretty well from view. She drew her hood closer around her face and lifted her pruning shears from her basket. One swift snip, two. Don't be selfish, just one more—

"Stop, thief," said a voice behind her. She spun and saw Robert Marne in handsome fawn corduroy. He looked alertly fresh and somehow exuding a pleased expectancy. A camera dangled by its strap from one hand.

"Surely you're not going to photograph me in the act?" cried Flora, forgetting to be furtive. The door of the stone cottage opened at the sound of her voice and a formidably tall dark woman came swiftly down the slate walk. She stared at Flora's handful of greenery and said, "Now look here—"

Robert moved to the wall and took the brunt of the woman's glare. "National Trust," he announced with authority. "An American grant in association with . . . well, you won't want to be bothered with the whole scheme. In any case, a study of rare and beautiful domestic English horticulture. May I compliment you on this fine specimen. We'd very much like your picture standing beside your *purpurea virgilii.*"

"Oh, is that the Latin for it?—we call it larkbush," the woman said, smiling now. She touched her hair. "Wait while I run in and do a bit of combing. I hadn't expected distinguished company at this hour."

While they waited, Flora said, "You are a perfect angel. And is that really the right name for this fine specimen, or did you make it up on the spot?"

"On the spot. Ah—here we are." Robert gravely took three shots of the shrub's owner, and then noted down her name and address with a promise to send her prints.

Why, Flora wondered, again charmed and amused by him, in fact delighted with him, was he being so out-of-his-way kind and nice? Was it always his manner? After all, she was just short of being a total stranger to him and here he was rescuing her in the most endearing fashion.

"Any more thefts in mind?" he asked as they walked along the herringboned bricks under fragrantly flowering pink hawthorn. "Or shall we wander and find some breakfast? Mine is usually coffee but for some reason I'm hungry. I see a promising signboard just down the street."

A small black car drew up beside them. Through the open window a girl's voice addressed Robert. She leaned toward him, short black hair spilling across one cheek. "Can you direct me to the Horsecollar—a pub or inn or whatever?"

"No, I'm afraid I can't, we're just passing through. Good luck." The car pulled away and Flora said, "That's where Denis is staying. After we down some breakfast I think I'll go in search of it myself and say good morning to Leo.''

Luce had no trouble at Gullion's in arranging an immediate departure on holiday. She had several weeks of it coming to her, and besides Ma Benson valued her. Not one of your casual comers-and-goers, but young as she was, a fixture, a feature, almost an institution at Gullion's. She held very well the drinks many men insisted on buying her, and was indeed a champion drink-stretcher, often the same half-full glass at her elbow for hours on end. A diversion at the bar was placing bets on how soon—two minutes, five?—she would swing her hair.

"If anyone asks specially tonight or tomorrow, the holiday's between me and you,'' Luce told Ma. "I don't want anyone tailing right after me, I want to be free and easy.'' "Silent as the grave,'' agreed Ma.

Luce went to Kennan's and hired herself a black Datsun. She had no idea where Tickell had gone for the day. Searching for work, perhaps. But the chances were that he'd be home to sleep. She went to the flat and packed a bag, left her note, and drove to Nanette's in Shepherd's Bush to spend the night. Nanette, in turn, was sworn to secrecy about the holiday.

At four-thirty in the morning, Luce got up, bathed and dressed, had a mug of instant coffee, and went down to her car. She'd figured the drive to Pym would take two hours or a little over, there certainly shouldn't be much traffic to contend with. She ought to be there by seven. She thought it unlikely that these rich sight-seeing Americans would hit the road as early as that. If they by any chance had, she would just take it from there.

Pym was not a large village, and after an unsuccessful inquiry as to the Horsecollar's whereabouts she found it five minutes later at the end of a lane. It was a ramblingly added-to brick building under three immense chestnut trees. The front door was still locked. But Luce, knowing the ways of hostelries, thought that surely there would be someone up and about at this hour. Behind-the-scenes work to be done, cooking to be started, and if the place was lazily run or shorthanded, last night's mess to be cleaned up.

She went around to her right and saw toward the back a row of windows lighted against the soft gray morning. Through a half-open door she heard a clattering of dishes, which stopped for a moment as a chicken was propelled out the door to shuffle squawking to several of its sisters by the wooden fence.

After a polite knock on the door, Luce went in to the kitchen. A large middle-aged woman was at the sink washing up. She had vacant blue eyes, an uncertain smile, and looked easily handle-able.

Luce glanced professionally around the room. "You run a nice kitchen here I must say. I work at Gullion's in London, Kensington, maybe you've dropped by there? Sister of the trade, you might say. You're the owner here, I shouldn't wonder.''

"No, just work here, but thanks anyway. How about some tea?'' Luce's opening statements had banished any doubts about the propriety of her thrusting herself into the kitchen in this way. "I'm Ida.''

"I'm Lucetta,'' said Luce. "I've come down here to see my boy, Denis Taunton. He's staying here, isn't he?''

Ida looked with wistful admiration at Luce's slender black pants, scarlet shirt, and slippery black hair, thinking how nice it must be to dash into any place at any hour to see your boy. And a handsome one he was, that Taunton fellow.

Tilting back her head to look at the ceiling, she said, "Probably still asleep. I don't hear a sound.'' The better to listen, she opened the door to the boxed-in back stairway. "Unless he's in the loo down the hall, a tub and shower there as well.''

Feeling suddenly in need of sustenance, Luce took her up on the offer of tea. "And you don't mind if I do myself a bit of toast?'' Ida hospitably made the toast and provided a choice of honey or jelly along with ample butter. Luce ate and drank, and now with the hollowness taken care of said, "I'll just run up and surprise him, shall I?'' Her smile had the quality of a wink. Ida thought again how nice it must be to have the nerve to surprise men sleeping in their beds or possibly emerging naked from their showers.

"Top of the stairs to the left," she directed in a tone of conspiracy. Luce ran up the stairs and stood listening at the closed door. There was a burst of falsetto barking from inside. She tried the knob. It turned accommodatingly and she pushed open the door. A poodle puppy backed away a little, still barking but with his puffball tail wildly wagging. She picked him up to quiet him and got an enthusiastic lick under her chin.

Denis with a dog, a poodle at that? Never. It must belong to his passengers.

She looked with another kind of hunger around the empty room. Tossed bed, the pillow at an angle, he always pulled his pillow about. Dark blue trousers and a jersey tossed over the back of a straight chair. One kicked-off shoe beside the bed, the other not in view. He was there in the air about her.

She went to a small table under a mirror and picked up his comb and combed her hair with it, studying her face. She looked all right, not tired even after getting up at that godawful hour.

Turning away from the mirror, she touched his dark blue jersey and astonished herself at the tenderness that swept her, the feeling of the stomach dropping away. She contemplated— partly need and partly strategy—taking off her clothes and waiting for him on the bed.

But, no. See what sort of reception she got first. He wasn't a predictable man. And without any clothes on you were . . . there was a right word for it beginning with a *v* but she couldn't bring it to mind and settled for defenseless.

The door opened and Leo leaped from his place on the bed beside her, onto the floor and up on his hind legs. Denis came in, in his white terry cloth robe she'd given him for his birthday.

He closed the door and stood leaning against it, studying her in silence under lowered eyelids. He didn't, he thought, have to ask her what she was doing here. Her pretext, over the telephone, had been, "He knows where to hunt for me. I need *you*."

After a moment, he said, "Do get the hell out of here, Luce."

She wished he wouldn't sound so calm about it, because underneath he couldn't be calm. She clung with a certain desperation to the idea of his paying her back, showing her—for a little while—that he could get along quite well without her, thanks.

With a snap of her shining hair, she said, "I've as much right to be in Pym as you have."

"Yes, but not in my room. Here, it's by invitation only."

A shock of rage reddened her face. She tried to push away the rage, it was only natural that he . . . wasn't it? Proud men didn't bend easily, didn't come running at the lift of a hand. "Look, Den, we've got to talk and straighten out a few things. No use shouting at each other over a high wall."

He looked at his watch. "Talk? I've got under ten minutes to dress and get out of here."

"Ten minutes is long enough for a lot of things. Tickell could hurt me, or worse, in ten seconds of time. All right, if you're in such a bloody hurry, where tonight can we pick it up again and clear the air one way or another?"

"I have no idea where garden-touring will land us tonight." Another door slammed in her face. All her inbred fighting instincts surged up under her ribs.

There was a knock at the door. Ida's voice said, "Not to interrupt, but there's a Mrs. Wallace downstairs wanting you, Mr. Taunton. Or especially the dog."

Denis reached for his trousers. "I'll bring him right down, tell her. Bye, Luce. Again."

"Until," said Luce.

NINE ❦ ❦ ❦

The lobby of the Carrack Arms at ten o'clock was a busy place, late breakfasters, check-ins and check-outs, anxious darts to the windows to see how heavily the rain was coming down, glances at the sky to hazard guesses at clearing.

Flora herself presented a one-woman bustle, sitting on a couch struggling to get on thin rubber boots over heavy crepe-soled shoes, her vigorous elbow sending her umbrella crashing to the floor every other minute. Leo, his leash handle about her wrist, interested himself in her boot problems and dashed busily back and forth at her feet.

"Denis," Flora said abstractedly to herself. "Where is Denis?" It was her morning practice to ensure reservations for the coming night before leaving present accommodations; or rather to have Denis do it. "Oh, there you are. And Robert too, all ready I see, as soon as I . . ."

In a corner, a woman asked her friend, "How

does an unbundled middle-aged female like that—my God, look at her hair coloring—get to have *two* awfully attractive men at her beck and call?" "Maybe she's rich," the friend said. "Or, and I think that's Marne, the film man, she might be an actress, but she'd certainly have to be a character actress."

Flora triumphantly managed the snaps of one boot. "The Haversham in Catchley, Denis. That way we'll get to see Mottisfont Abbey—and get a peek at the rock gardens at Hardings Lacey—as well as Mulsey House. Perhaps we'll leave Stourhead for tomorrow, the rain will slow us up. Good morning, Emily dear."

Emily had breakfasted in her room, thinking as she was doing so, Am I hiding? The answer was yes. How demeaning, hiding from Robert. And, how comforting and relaxing. Now they would by stages work their way to Mulsey House, Robert would look over his water-lily pond, and then no doubt would be off on his way, to attend to other chores having to do with his film on the bad behavior of Mrs. Blessingham.

Second boot snapped, Flora, short of breath from the battle, gasped, "Robert, will you be staying the night with us? I mean, near Mulsey House in case you need several days of research or whatever it is you do on the scene?"

"Yes," Robert said, and to Denis, "Add me to your roster if you will."

A round rosy woman in Shetland tweeds came over to Emily, who was perched raincoated on the arm of the couch. With no attempt to lower her well-bred voice, she said to Emily and the lobby, nodding at the large vase of long-stemmed white roses she was carrying, "These were brought to my room by mistake last night, they mistook Denton for Denver. I rang the desk but you were out, so I put the poor dears in water and then, what do you know, I fell asleep. So here, belatedly, sorry, and"—reaching into her jacket pocket—"a note."

The roses were from Otis. He had made her promise to call him every third day and yesterday she had called him and told him where they would be staying that night. "All love, darling," said the note. "Let's move it up to August. Or better still July. You do leave an echoing blank behind you."

She knew from old Robert's ability to read upside down at racing speed, but when she looked up from the note his eyes were gazing innocently over her head.

"Roses o'er the ocean," he said. "In several ways an extravagance. Doesn't he know you're up to your navel in flowers all day? I'd say your—Otis, is it?—is a bit out of touch."

As there was no convenient way to carry the roses in the car, however much their scented white beauty was disparaged and dismissed by Robert, Emily took the vase of offered endearments to the desk and was thanked for them. "Just right with the white stock I'll be cutting later," the woman behind the desk said.

It was when they were a few miles away from Hardings Lacey, described in Flora's notes as "a wondrous half acre of jeweled alpines and ancient little bonsai trees," that Denis noticed what seemed to be a patiently following car, a black Datsun.

Leaving the Horsecollar, he had noticed the car parked in front, by all odds Luce's: a black Datsun. Common enough make, but—

"Until," Luce had said in that warble of hers.

When they stopped at the little hutch at the gate where you paid the attendant and signed the visitors' book, Flora said hopefully to Robert, "Even in the rain, surely you'd like to see this? There's said to be a very high rock at the top, almost a little cliff, that someone in your movie might throw himself off." Already, she found his company quite the pleasantest thing humanly speaking that had happened since her arrival in England. After Emily's, of course.

Robert declined with thanks and asked for her book of poetry to divert himself with. Emily had no desire for a soaking, but the cost of remaining dry, more or less alone with Robert in the Gaspard, sent her up the rain-spongy grass paths among the rocks and flowers and bonsais. The foot-high trees, so nobly scaled in their old, trained perfection, made her feel not at all godlike. Instead, looking down at them or encountering a miniature grove at eye level, gave her a sense of being somehow herself monstrous,

95

lost, out of scale with the earth, the world. Right at the moment, they were bad-dream trees.

She must call Otis tonight and thank him for his roses. Yes, call Otis. Otis? Who was he? Blame it on the bonsais, the frightening unreality of him, the face, the body, fading bonelessly into the drifts of rain.

Coming upon a little trelliswork gazebo with a fairy-tale mosaic-mirror roof, she took refuge inside on a bench and sat shivering a little, bare cold hands clasped together in her lap. Hurry, Flora, hurry. So that I can get out of this unnerving place and back . . . back to what?

There was an almost soundless step behind her and something light and warm was thrown over her shoulders. The step was Denis's, coming in from an arched opening at the back of the gazebo, and so was the jacket, dark blue quilted over a puffy lining.

"You're cold," he said. He reached down and touched the back of one of her clenched hands. "Right to your fingertips."

"Very kind of you, thank you, Denis." The politeness, a trifle awkward, perhaps because the quilted jacket warming her gave the strange effect of a near-caress.

"Not at all kind. Don't you know that women obviously in love attract other males like bees?"

"I'm not in love," Emily said indignantly, looking up into the blue eyes, the face bending close. And then with dismay, "At least, right now, all that's . . . he's . . . a long way away . . ."

Why would any near-stranger have been examining her so closely? Or was it there for all the world, for Flora, for even the waitress at last night's dinner, for *Robert,* to see and smile at?

Obviously in love. What did you do in this frightful nakedness? Go into emotional and physical purdah? Hide yourself behind yourself?

To return to the worst of it, if Denis the newcomer on the scene had spotted it, what about Robert, who knew her, all about her, every expression, every flick of an eyelash, every smallest movement of the hand? How shaming, how disastrous—my poor cast-off darling all aflutter again. "Oh hell, in all conscience I'd better give her a day or so more of my time." Throw her a bone, throw her a presence in the car. Be nice, sound affectionate, speaking of the past beside a twilit pond.

Where was armor, or shelter, or escape to be found during these few kindly given days of his? Plead an obscure pain (and horribly enough it was that). A recurrence, say, of throat trouble or some mysterious private female ailment, and flee back to New York instantly, for medical help? "I wouldn't be comfortable with anyone but my own doctor in a matter like this." Leave Flora cold.

And at the same time signal to Robert, It is unbearable to me to be near you in this, as must be plain to you, pathetic and laughable condition. Good-bye again and forever.

An immense black umbrella held at a slant to the east against the rain preceded Flora, who now appeared at the front archway of the gazebo. She came in, shaking the umbrella and her raincape in the thorough-going manner of a very large dog.

"But they say it's good for the skin," she panted. "God's own Elizabeth Arden salon. The ground was so wet that one or two magenta saxifrage—very rare—had all but worked themselves loose from their rock so I rescued them." She tapped the straw basket on her arm.

Bursting with happiness at all the little wonders she had seen, she showed no surprise at the tête-à-tête, at Emily with Denis's jacket over her shoulders.

When they got back to the car Emily noticed that Robert's raincoat was wet, and his hair too, curling around his ears and nape as it always did in the rain. Did he still spurn umbrellas? Had he tired of his poetry, or been taking Leo out for an emptying? In any case, of no moment: just stop all Robert-reacting. Even though, until a little while back, she had been unaware of eagerly watching, listening, taking him in through every pore.

Denis started the engine with a glance in the driving mirror. There was a tight curve behind the verge where he had stopped. The black Datsun had either sheltered there during the garden visit or had gone innocently on. And perhaps it was only his imagination that it was Luce following them. The blurred windscreen and the sweep of the wipers had made the driver's face a dim uncertainty. But, don't leave the doubt dangling.

He swung the car off the main road into a steeply climbing lane, its ten-foot-high stone retaining walls green with moss and little ferns and spilling vines and flowers. Before Flora could get a proper look at this wall garden made by the years and the winds he took another turning into a rutted dirt road half-circling a pond full of mallards enjoying the downpour. Then left again up a hill to a little gray stone church dressed in ivy. The narrow road merely made a loop around the church. Denis stopped the car at the front steps.

"Someone wanting to pay devotions?" Robert asked. How city-metallic he sounded, Emily thought, how almost harsh, for no reason she could imagine. "Or—if this was an old movie or a third-rate new one—I thought," addressing Denis, "you thought there might be a car following us."

Denis opened the door and said over his shoulder, "Left rear tire feels a bit off, I'll just check it."

Bending to the faultless tire, he cast an eye down the hill. About halfway to the bottom there was a stone house set well back from the road, thick ivy-woven hollies heavily bordering what must be its driveway. She could have seen, just in time, the car stopping at the church at the top of the hill, and nipped into the drive. Intruding, trespassing, was no problem to the Luces of the world—"Is this the Trents' house? I was told, on the way up the little road to the church. Could I have the wrong church?"

Flora, who had implicit trust in Denis's command of the wheel, the route, and the habits and manners of the Gaspard, said as he got back into the car, "Had you wanted us to see this pretty church? The sign on the door says it's open just for Evensong and Sunday services."

"Just a thought," Denis answered, which Robert considered no answer at all. "And anyway the road beyond Hardings Lacey is torn up for repairs, they told me at the petrol station this morning."

They headed back down the hill. As they neared the duck pond at the bottom he saw in the mirror the Datsun emerge from its sheltering hollies.

Okay, Luce, he said to himself, follow along and to hell with you. For the time being.

He could hardly stop the car, walk back to hers, challenge her on the road and—observed and probably overheard by his three passengers —order her out of this and home.

Luce didn't take kindly to orders. Even from him.

Even when his order had been, It's all over, Luce. Forget it.

TEN

No point in haring off after a plum-colored custom-made car and its driver if what he wanted, what he had to get his hands on, had been left behind in Luce's flat.

Tickell, humming "Sing, Sing a Song," searched with a swift and refined efficiency, first the flat and then the boxroom. It wasn't anywhere, his gold case. The only small reward was a Polaroid color shot of a man in a dark blue jersey, his hair tossed in the wind. The photograph was tucked into a family album Luce's dead mum had kept. There was nothing written on the back to identify the man, but Tickell felt in his wary bones that it was probably Denis Taunton.

He looked, yes, like the kind Luce might talk about in her sleep. And the snap had an odd immediacy, a right-now feel about it.

With a nervous eye on the clock, Tickell packed

a small canvas bag with what would be enough, hope and pray, for two or three days at most. He took off the suit in which a respectable man could make a respectable inquiry at a car-rental company, and put on dark trousers and a zipped brown vinyl jacket over a heavy plaid shirt. It would be a chilly trip and wet too, he wouldn't be surprised.

He took the Underground to Hammersmith and walked a few blocks to his destination on the Great West Road. It was a shabby shop with a yard and shed behind, and a sign proclaiming in faded red letters, "Vane's Cycle Repair. Buy & Sell. Also Rentals."

"I see they've let you loose to prey on the innocent again," Harry Vane said with a grin. "Welcome home, Tick." They had known each other for twenty years.

And that was all the time wasted in idle conversation. Tickell stated his needs and produced the cash to pay for them. He chose a muddied motorcycle, not new, not old, not showy, just a way of getting around on two fast wheels. He rented a helmet and goggles. He was issued a license in the name of Ernest Dawson. He strapped the canvas bag onto his machine and within twenty-five minutes of entering Vane's was on his way on the Great West Road, no one you'd take the extra trouble to glance at.

Just a skilled, law-abiding cyclist, going the maximum allowed speed but no faster. Exhibiting no bold flair or style in the handling of what was often a vehicle arrogantly used.

The rain started, at first soft and thin. It blurred his goggles and he had to take them off. He found himself in a state of intense nervousness, wanting to up his speed and get there—get where? Wherever the man in the Gaspard was going next, from the Horsecollar at Pym.

The photograph he had found in the album appeared before his eyes. The face, the big long-fingered hands. He saw a hand flicking the catch on the gold case, the eyes lingering on the scratches that might or might not be a map. The pictured man had a look of having his wits about him.

This part of the trip, going southwest from London, was like rerunning an old film. Given to caution in all his undertakings, he had paid a lone visit to Spill two days before the robbery, to look over the geographical situation in general. Size of the town, density of the houses near the Gadneys' place, location of the police station. And, in case of alarm or pursuit or anything going wrong a hide-hole, an escape hatch. It had been during this careful survey that he had come upon the burned-out house with its overgrown drive, on its lonely road, deep woods stretching beyond.

Even then, even that Sunday, he had wished it was a one-man job, himself and nobody else. But the information had come from Yore. And there were the two separate locations to hit, the main house and the brick cottage the mother-in-law lived in. Taking turns, one would watch and listen while the other worked—for a wandering dog beginning to bark, for a cruising police car, for a visitor who didn't know the Gadneys were out; or for a member of the family unexpectedly coming home with, say, a sick stomach.

He didn't know Yore all that well, he wasn't an old close friend but an acquaintance of only six months or so. All he did know was that Yore gave an impression of extreme efficiency: He had never been caught at any of the various projects he successfully carried through. Had never, unlike Tickell, seen the inside of a prison. Younger than Tickell, powerful too, no nerves ever observed ruffling the stolid surface.

It had been going well and smoothly, Tuesday night. There were no resident dogs to worry about; according to Kemp the gardener, Mr. Gadney, coming home very late and very drunk one night, had been attacked by his own guard dog, and that was the end of that.

It was a dark cold night of fog and rain, chilling but helpful, a night for most people to stay at home. The lock had yet to be invented which could outclass Tickell's skills; and he had no trouble at all with the combination of the safe, again thanks to Kemp. He shoveled everything on its shelves into his plastic lawn-clippings bag, holding in his mouth his pencil flash. He swiftly rejoined Yore in the car, which was pulled deep in under trees in the lane around the corner. They drove along the lane and turned left into Gulliver

Road, which the brick cottage faced from a distance of forty yards or so.

Waiting in the car, Tickell thought Yore was taking a hell of a long time. Don't push our luck, chum. He sank deeper in the seat as headlights showed an approaching car, cutting speed. But it was only slowing to turn in to the lane. Would curious eyes catch a vague glisten of a car without lights, parked close to the vine-covered fence?

No longer able to sit still, he opened the car door and got out. He heard himself humming and stopped it. What was that noise from the field on the other side of Gulliver Road? Just a tree branch groaning as the wet wind picked up?

Listening toward the field, his back to the fence, he was struck on the head by a heavy blow from behind. He staggered forward, fell on one shoulder, and righting himself, finding his feet, he perceived rather than saw Yore. There was no process of thought involved for the next few seconds.

He reached into an inner raincoat pocket, seized his knife and plunged at Yore. Save himself, pay Yore back, it didn't matter where the knife hit as long as it hurt. Yore made a strangled screaming sound and pitched forward, almost knocking Tickell down again.

Another car went by, fortunately at over-the-limit speed, stereo shrieking through an open window. The driver too drunk, maybe, to catch a glimpse of two men, one standing and one fallen, on the other side of the parked car. The next driver to come along might be stone sober.

Tickell opened the back door of the car and half lifted, half shoved Yore into it, any which way, seat, floor, it didn't matter. During this swift operation, he had stumbled over something heavy: Yore's takings. One lawn-clipping bag, another bag that felt like canvas, unexpectedly heavy, with awkward corners of something inside it which whacked Tickell on a shin. But the pain at the time went unnoticed.

He started the car, making a U-turn on Gulliver Road which would lead them in another direction than that of the center of the little town of Spill. Was Yore alive, there in back? Did it matter? Get the two of them out of here fast—

He was going to leave me there, lying there, take off with the whole works, Tickell thought incredulously. Epithets for Yore, none of them bad enough, poured through his racing mind. *And what could I have done about it afterward? Nothing.*

Except try in some way to pay the bastard back.

But . . . let's see . . . He shook his head to clear his mind of a strange blurring, maybe that fist of Yore's behind his ear had been responsible for it . . .

But he'd already done that. Paid him back.

There was no sound from the back of the car.

Was Yore just waiting silently there, playing mum, not wanting to attack the driver from behind while the car was in motion? The back of Tickell's neck had a cold crawl over it.

Or would he give an unthinking wild-beast spring?

"You're okay, you're all right," Tickell said aloud to Yore in a voice that was meant to be soothing, and frightened himself by whatever kind of idiocy his voice was conveying.

Oh Christ, a car right behind him. Might Yore be signaling, or presenting a frantic bloodied face at the rear window? The car passed him and in its headlights Tickell saw a road sign, Xavier Road, and even in his panic recollection worked like the combination of the Gadney safe.

A minute later he turned the car in to the weedy driveway of the burned-out house. He stopped, now completely shielded from the road by the willow grove in front. With his pencil flash, he took a look at Yore. Eyes, Jesus, open. Would that mean he—?

Tickell with shuddering fingers felt for the heart and saw his own gloved hand covered with, dripping with, blood. He took his hand hastily away. What else? Oh—pulse. Nothing. He bent and muttered to the twisted open-eyed face, "Yore. Yore. *Yore!*"

Nothing.

Tickell had never before killed, but death proclaimed itself to him in an unmistakable fashion.

Had he, without thinking about it, aimed for the heart, then? There was no way to remember and no way to know, ever.

Yore had taken off his raincoat before leaving the car for the brick cottage and wore only a dark shirt which all but concealed the spreading wet. Would the raincoat have blunted the thrust and saved his life? What did that matter, now?

There was another blur. Tickell, returning from it, found he had lost all sense of time and place. Where . . . ? He switched on his flash again, shielding it with cupped fingers which glowed a faint red, but this was living blood, in this hand. He saw dimly, to his left, the stone well.

Only fifteen yards or so, but it felt three times that, dragging Yore's body through the long grass, the brambles. He pried off the well cover with his knife, and grunting with the effort got the upper half of Yore over the edge, lifted the rest of him, and sent him downward. He threw the knife in after him.

The splash of the body hitting the water seemed frighteningly quick to his ears. Or was that just time, seconds or so, playing tricks on him, was it really a long, safe way down? A man of cities, he knew nothing about wells. In rainy seasons, did they rise like tides? What if the body floated up (it would, of course) and was visible to anyone casually looking into the well?

He remembered the peculiarly heavy cloth bag Yore had been carrying along with the plastic bag. His shin still hurt where a poking-out corner of something had hit it. He went to the car, lifted out the cloth bag, hearing himself panting now, gasping, feeling it was all he could do to breathe. He threw the bag down the well, where it might or might not land on top of and anchor Yore. After all, the well's diameter was only about five feet.

Anything else that needed to be thrown in? Yes, his bloodied gloves. And go back to the car for Yore's raincoat. The pockets of this were suspiciously bulging but he didn't dare take the time to go through them and turn them out. Particularly as the sounds from the woods were getting worse, swishings and groanings, nothing but the wind in the trees, but still—splash went the raincoat.

He drove northeast, to Heathrow. He considered trying to find a space in a metered parking section of the immense air terminus, but now he was shivering, exhausted, and frightened by every sight and sound. Instead, he pulled the Volkswagen behind the run-down shack of an out-of-business petrol station with a cracked oily concrete apron and a "For Sale" sign in front.

There was a suitcase in the trunk, provided by Yore, who made the reasonable point that, unless there was a garbage truck nearby, men with plastic bags in hand looked odd on London streets no matter how late the hour. He dumped the contents of both bags into the suitcase and walked to the Heathrow Central Underground station, a man with a suitcase among countless other luggage-carrying persons.

Luce was away, at her brother's in Barkingside, which was just as well, nobody to face, no tales, false, to have to tell.

Safely arrived at the flat and drinking whiskey, a great deal of it, he pushed aside for a while his rage at Yore, who had been going to dump him and run, and who had made him do this, all of this. Rage was a dangerous thing, it could undo the stitching that held you together.

Instead, he allowed himself careful congratulations. Naturally they would never find Yore. He had left his stolen car near Heathrow and gone off somewhere by plane. Forged papers were no problem to the Yores of London.

But wait. Better still, if the car ever caught official eyes, there was no earthly reason to connect an old, stolen Volkswagen with anybody in particular. Just a nameless thief. If, that is, it was even glanced at, behind the extinct petrol station.

Reading in his newspaper the next day the account of the robbery at Spill, Tickell found that what he had thrown down the well to weight Yore at the bottom was approximately fifty thousand pounds worth of gold.

ELEVEN

There were two people serving at the busy bar of the Horsecollar. A short monkey-faced man at one end and an amply built middle-aged woman at the other, with faded blond hair and blue eyes that looked a little vague. Tickell, wet and tired and thirsty, thought he'd try her first.

He ordered a pint of bitter and asked her what she'd have, and then inquired about his friend Denis Taunton. He had been, he said, supposed to meet him at the bar here, had she seen him?

Ida giggled, saluting him with her small shot of gin. "He's a popular man, someone else came to see him, this morning, early—maybe you know her, Lucetta, her name was. His girl, I suppose—" She stopped and flushed. "But I shouldn't be . . . no, he's not here. He left a bit after ten this morning with his dog. Or not his, hers . . . a woman who . . ." Feeling rather lost in these complicated details, she applied herself to the remainder of her gin.

"Did he leave here in his car? Or just walk off, or what?"

"No, he was carrying his bag, he checked out, I know because I had to make up the room fresh."

"Well, he said he was driving—where do you suppose his car was? I might be able to catch him up from . . ."

"I don't know, perhaps on the street somewhere near. There's a parking garage though, you go down the lane and turn right at the High Street, and it's only a block or so."

Tickell didn't think you'd leave a car as valuable as the Gaspard sounded sitting at any old curb. He thanked her and finished his bitter in two swallows. Then, remembering his surface excuse for this roam, he thought he'd better leave a visible footprint at the Horsecollar and added, with his tilted smile, "She's my girl, too, the one this morning. A lark's okay, but—well, you know, don't you dear."

Two men at once, Ida thought wistfully. She smiled and said, "Oh, I do. You men—you keep us hopping!"

"By the way," as he laid a coin for her beside his glass, "What car was she driving when she turned up this morning?"

"There was a black—I don't know a lot about cars but I think it was a Datsun, Japanese anyway—in front, under the tree. I think that'd be hers."

The ancient attendant at the parking garage

didn't want to be bothered with vehicles gone from his immediate scene until Tickell produced a pound note. "I've got to get in touch with him, a business matter."

The attendant bethought himself. "His tank was almost empty when I brought the car out. I told him, in case he hadn't noticed, and he asked where the nearest petrol station was. I asked him which direction he was going and he said west and asked the best road to a place called Hardings Lacey. I told him the Exxon station was on his road just toward the end of the town."

Up the street from the garage was a card and gift shop. Tickell went in and asked a pleasant gray-haired woman if she had a guide to gardens that were open to the public. She gave him, in his helmet and goggles and zipped jacket, a rather surprised glance, and then reminded herself that in England the most unlikely people were passionate gardeners.

He didn't look to be in the market for any of her large handsome books with color plates. She found a nice paperback for him crammed with maps and information. "Is it this particular vicinity you're interested in?"

"No, all over, but of course while I'm here . . . would you mark some places for me? I'm going roughly west."

"Well, let's see. You mustn't miss Hardings Lacey, surely the most beautiful rock garden in England, and then . . ." Busy with her pen, she rattled off name after name, Stourhead,

113

Mottisfont Abbey, Lytes Cary, Mulsey House. And on and on. Oh God, Tickell thought. At least a bloody week's work of gardens, it sounded.

But so far he'd been lucky. Not only lucky, but his instincts, his nerve ends, had been right.

Maybe you know her, Lucetta her name was.

Three things simplified his search. The rain had stopped and the gray skies lifted higher and brighter. He had the Gaspard in his mind's eye, a car that would silently trumpet its presence in any roadside queue, any car park at any grand stately-home garden, so that it would not be necessary to make his way through acres of blossoms to see if he could spot his man. And he had the name Mrs. Wallace; although he found that here you had to sign the visitors' book and there you didn't have to, when you paid your fee for entering.

Having scanned this car park and that queue, you found you had no need to pay for entrance. No Gaspard. Unless there were privileged ways in, for special cars with special people in them, rich. Lord and Lady Something-or-Other: "But don't park with the crowd. Do come in at the front drive and leave your car in our garage."

Thrust that away, too discouraging, tempting you to say, Oh, the hell with this, get back to London, get your backpacking gear together and get on with it, down the well at Spill.

But, the fingernail on the catch of the gold case, lid flying up, and whatever kind of brain it was under the dark wind-blown hair, puzzling . . . Are these the initials of names of roads somewhere? What is this little circle?

It was shortly after four-thirty that, following discreet finger-post signs, he turned in through the tall open wrought-iron gates into the car park of Mulsey House, at the far rear of the property. Business was not brisk this afternoon. There were only six other cars besides the plum-and-cream Gaspard.

Tickell drew up his motorcycle at the other end of the row of cars and glanced through their windows. He could make out a man at the wheel of the Gaspard, head bent, asleep? No, there was a book open on the steering wheel. The man in the Polaroid shot. Denis Taunton in person, and not thirty feet away.

Another car came in and took the empty place on his left. There was a chatter of women's voices through its window. Well, this wouldn't have been the right place, anyway, too much coming and going, and you didn't just walk up to a stranger and say, "You've got something of mine. Please give it back."

What in fact did you do? Tickell hadn't thought his way through to that. The iron necessity came first, the method would follow.

The man at the wheel turned his head at the sound of the high chattering. Tickell instinctively bent his own helmeted head down to inspect his front wheel. But there were no photographs of him anywhere in Luce's apartment, he'd found that out as a sort of fringe benefit of this morning's search. Denis Taunton could have no

115

idea of what he looked like. And if Luce for some reason had ever described him to Taunton, what was there to say? All-right looking . . . not tall . . . brown eyes . . . proud of his sterling-silver hair, though.

The hair was completely concealed under the helmet.

He hadn't the patience just to sit there, waiting. The sign at the gate entrance said the hours for seeing over the gardens were from two to six. Taunton's party might linger until closing time. And their driver might tire of his book and look about for someone to chat with.

He got off his motorcycle and strolled to the little green-and-white striped ticket booth, immediately behind the three just-arrived women. One of them turned to him and said, "Oh, there you are," and Tickell's heart jumped briefly. "Right on time." To her companions, she said, "This is Mr. Cyril Cosby, from the county Garden Society, who when I telephoned him kindly offered to be our guide. Only, I was under the impression you'd be bicycling—aren't you dashing, with your motorcycle?"

"Sorry," he said. A trap of some kind? Impossible. Or was it? "My name is"—just remembering in time—"Dawson."

She looked over his shoulder and said, "Ah, there is our man on his bicycle, he must be . . ." and Tickell rapidly paid the young woman at the booth his fifty-pence admission fee. He started to climb a winding path and a split-second

116

reconnaissance told him where to go. The path divided almost immediately; he took the hill-climbing one to the left. At the top of the hill there was a little green-painted bench, thoughtfully placed so that the sore-footed or physically hampered could, just after getting out of their cars, sample the splendors of Mulsey House. A downward sweep of velvet green, walled mightily on one side with oak and chestnut, a graceful distant rise to an Ionic-columned marble temple, and from islands of willows in the undulating green a windblown silver glistening of fountains.

If you turned your head right around the other way, you saw through monkey-puzzle trees the car park almost directly below.

Tickell sat down on the bench and in order to present a natural sort of picture to any unseen inquiring eye devoted himself for a few minutes to his garden handbook. Then he took from his pocket a monocular. He allowed another minute of thoughtful study to the Ionic temple, and then swiveled around.

He couldn't have told himself in so many words what he was looking for, but he found it.

There hadn't been a black Datsun in the car park. But the monocular brought him one, drawn well in on the grass verge beside the stone wall, a good way down the road from the wrought-iron gates. While he watched, Luce got out of the car, and leaning against it lit a cigarette. And yawned.

What the *hell?* She couldn't be following him,

Tickell, to warn and protect her precious Denis? But she couldn't have an earthly idea of where he was or what he was up to.

He tried to find a likelier, more acceptable possibility. She'd be joining him tonight, wherever he would be staying, and was just patiently standing by while he got through his day's work. That must be it.

Christ, after they all left this place, he'd have to cope with following behind her as well as the Gaspard. It wouldn't do to serve as a sort of unofficial escort between the two cars.

Funny the man in the Gaspard wouldn't wander back and treat himself to a hug or kiss or something or other. He was still at the wheel.

Now there was another car on his far side, a tan Ford Cortina, with a man sitting in that one too, bent sideways studying a road map on the seat. Tickell put his monocular away and opened his handbook again. She couldn't possibly, from that distance, see him through the leaves and branches, high on his hill. He was, for the moment, okay.

"I'll come along with you for a bit, Robert," Flora said, "and see if the lily pond suits you. Then, when the movie comes out, what nice memories."

"I'm off to the Rose Hoop," Emily said, "or that's what it's called in your notes."

They were well along the rising then dipping asphalted path that led from the car park. Robert cast an eye at the gray and white unruly clouds.

"I hope," he said, "that if it starts to rain again your man Denis will take appropriate action as he did back at Hardings, and come and find you. If you're to be found."

He gave her a look she had not been subjected to—or treated to—in three years, an intimate searching survey right down through her own eyes to the marrow of her bones.

Emily would have sought out any desperately uninteresting goal to get away from his disturbing presence—the garden waterworks system, for instance, or the enclosed yards of prize poultry—but the Rose Hoop rewarded her for a time. The perimeters were swags of roses hung between slender garlanded posts, with a turfed circle inside and in the center an ordered explosion of color and perfume, each rose identified.

In a bemused way, she read some of the harmonious tag names, Blessings, Michele Meilland, Violinsta Costa, Lilli Marlene, Sarabande, Danse de Feu, Souvenir de Malmaison.

She was alone here, and thought she had better move on. He might come looking for her, knowing where she was. The eyes curiously brilliant and raking, over the words "your man Denis." She could only assume that, strolling in the rain, he had observed and misinterpreted the little scene in the gazebo.

My poor dear Emily, is it a matter now of anyone in sight?

Following a habit of years, she started to walk,

very fast, after leaving the roses; it didn't really matter in what direction. To clear the head, steady the breathing, feel the reassurance of the physical rhythm, the body working well, nothing wrong with you at all—nothing wrong with Emily.

Had the hard restless walking, which had started when Robert ended, been a form of running away? Running from the center of things to the safe faraway edges?

Nonsense. Walk to where you'll get your balance back, get yourself back. Don't just sit and simmer like a pudding. In her haste, she turned to look behind her and wandered straight into the green down-drifting fronds of a weeping willow. But there was no one following.

She heard a swish and rustle as a form—a man's—moved toward her through the masking hanging ribbons of leaves. She paused on a caught-in breath and then saw not who it was but who it wasn't.

A pale young man in a dirty raincoat, his dark eyes nervous. "Pardon me, have you seen a man around, wearing a helmet? Motorcyclist?"

"No, sorry."

"That's all right, sorry to bother you but . . ." words inconclusively dying away as he passed her, going almost at a lope up toward the Rose Hoop.

Emerging from another arc of weeping willows, she saw Flora a distance below. She was sitting on a graceful little bench beside what must be Robert's pool, which lay at the foot of gentle slopes. Flora lifted her arm in a beckoning wave.

"He thought it was just right," she announced, with happy enthusiasm. "They'd have to install a fountain, and bring in rocks to make a ledge. He must have shot at least two rolls of film, wandering all around. I do like to see professionals at work, wrapped up in themselves —knowing exactly what they're doing. Such a rare sight these days."

Then he really was working on Mrs. Blessingham. What (wasn't it?) a relief to find that the project was not a mysterious invention, a way of briefly prolonging a chance meeting, when they had, as he had also mysteriously said, "so little time." Ghosts, and drifts and devils of doubt, were sent scattering in this gray practical light.

Flora bent down to rub her ankle. "Emily dear, will you do something for me, go up to the house and see if they serve tea? Most of these places do. But I'd like to save a wasted walk if no tea's to be had. Somewhere today I took a wrong step and my ankle's talking back to me."

A series of terraced gardens hedged in yew led upward to the silvery stone of the long graceful Palladian front. No need, any longer, to glance out of the corner of an eye for any sign of Robert. He had bowed himself out of questions, of intrigue.

The old, gilded knocker on the tall white door was a circle of cherubs' heads and wings. Emily lifted it and let it fall and after a suitable formal wait of about forty seconds the door was opened by a butler. Did people really have butlers anymore? Perhaps he was just a form of stage prop, hired for days when the house was open to paying visitors. He stood aside and she entered a long wide reception hall, and was unrewarded in a twenty-foot-high mirror by the sight of a wind-tossed woman in a raincoat, her damp hair every which way, her nose pink from the cold, the dark rims of her glasses the only orderly part of the picture.

"I wondered—" For God's sake don't sound so timid, the size of the hall drinking up the ordinary speaking voice. Louder. "Are teas served here, that is, to people who come to see the house and gardens?"

"Sorry, madam, no. The house, as a matter of fact, is not open to visitors except during the month of August. The tickets at present are only for the gardens," the butler informed her loftily. You are intruding, madam, and as soon as you intrude yourself out the door the better. He moved to put a hand on the knob.

How could you, at the age of thirty-four, be made to feel like a child caught stealing apples in somebody's orchard? These pushy Americans—

A tall paneled pale green door to the right of the mirror was halfway open. Through it came Robert, with a martini in his hand, and a remarkably pretty girl sprung whole from the latest issue of *Vogue:* doeskin knee-breeches, creamy rumpled boots, an immense hairy Missoni sweater of orange and mauve, and powdered red hair with an Alexander Hamilton bow at the neck.

Robert looked for a fleeting moment startled and discomposed. "I heard your voice—is there anything the matter?"

"No, I just was asking if there was a place, a public room, for tea here, Flora . . ." Don't bring up Flora and her ankle, with the implied suggestion that Mulsey House must find the heart to take two waifs in out of the cold and the wind.

The horrible thought struck her that Robert might easily conclude that she was pursuing him, up terraces and through closed doors, anything to keep him in her sight, the little while she had him around. And so she missed part of his introductions.

". . . Donna Corcoran, BBC, or perhaps you guessed that." Did one of his eyes narrow into a secret near-wink? "We both happened to be working in Rome about a year ago, on different jobs. And then she . . ."

Donna Corcoran took a healthy swig of her martini and interrupted, "I was looking out a window and I saw this poor damp darling wandering about with his camera, looking absolutely starved for gin and sympathy. I'm staying here for the weekend, with Mummy and her, what? fourth? Lovely to meet you, what was the name again, darling?"

"My wife," Robert said.

There was a short three-part silence. Emily

dimly heard the butler, six feet away, clear his throat.

"How odd it is that you think you know people so terribly well and don't actually know them at all," the BBC girl said in a clear high voice. "Won't you join us for a drink, Mrs. Marne?"

"Thanks, no, I must . . . I have a friend waiting patiently for me down by the pond." She could manage no more, no good-bye, nice to have met you. She turned and walked to the door and opened it before the butler could reach the knob again.

To Flora, she said, "Tea's out, the house is closed to trippers. Let's go along now, without Robert. I assume he's working out details with the owners about using this place as a background for Mrs. Whatever."

"All right, we'll find tea in the town, I do need it." Flora got up and tested her ankle. "Better, only a little throbby." Then she added, in a curious reverse quote to that just uttered in the hall, "Knowing Robert—although I really don't but feel somehow I do—he'll find his way back to us one way or another."

TWELVE

The Haversham at Catchley was an agreeable tall huddle of three joined sixteenth-century black-and-white houses, directly on the cobbled street, with its lawns and gardens behind. Denis dropped off Emily, Flora, and Leo, the Haversham having no objection to pets in rooms, and waited while the suitcases were taken out of the trunk. As usual, he would go on to more casual accommodations, whatever he could find on the spur of the moment.

This was not a matter of economizing, as his hotel arrangements were paid for by his passengers, but personal taste on his part. "I like unbuttoned places at night," he had told Flora. She thought, as he got back into the car in front of the Haversham, that he could have come over quite convincingly as lord and master of, say, Hardings Lacey, in the proper tweeds.

The Gaspard drove off into the cold purpling

light cast by low clouds heavy with rain, and the fateful ballet began.

Denis drove slowly down the High Street and took a right turn into another amply built-over thoroughfare, Queen's Way. Go along a bit, until it starts to get shabby, with gaps and open yards between the buildings.

Luce followed behind him, three cars back, a presence of which he was well aware. Separated again by a three-car length, the motorcycle dawdled, ridden by a nobody man in a brown vinyl jacket, dark trousers, helmet, and goggles. There was only one car and a bus between the motorcycle and the tan Ford which had been parked beside the Gaspard at Mulsey House.

Just where the shabby stretch of Queen's Way was beginning to smarten up a bit, Denis saw a large shambling brick building which called itself in green neon the Imperial, only the final L was unlighted. Ought to feel homey, Denis thought—yet another empire down the drain. He pulled into the car park at the right, found one of the few remaining spaces, and left and locked the car. If the Imperial had a room for him, he'd register, have a drink, and then see to a more secure night's resting place for the car.

There was evidently a salesmen's convention in full swing at the hotel, and they'd all have to be on the unsuccessful side, Denis thought, eyeing the gray faces, the paunches, the assertive but rumpled clothing. The public bar to the right was doing a brisk business, and the lounge to the left busy too, mostly women, the salesmen's wives, no doubt.

It wasn't his milieu but he found it fleetingly amusing and at the desk asked for and obtained a room on the third floor. There were no imperial attendants to usher him upward. He was given a key after he signed the register card. He picked up his duffle bag and went to one of two old noisily gasping elevators.

Luce entered the lobby as the elevator doors slid together. With luck she might not, later, need a room of her own, but best to hedge your bets. Besides, she was tired and wanted a freshening up and a change of clothes. "You just made it, duck," the desk clerk told her. "Last and only one we've got."

"I'm to meet a friend, Denis Taunton. What's his room number, please?" It was 3G, down the hall from her 3F. Funny, the clerk thought, she doesn't look the type for separate rooms when meeting a friend.

Tickell stood smoking in the street, watching her through the glass door, until she entered the elevator. Then he went in to the desk and found himself turned down. The clerk looked him over and suggested with a faint grin, "There's a place across the street, the Bell and Bonnet, more expensive than we are but . . ."

Tickell thought he'd have a drink before he tried the Bell and Bonnet. His back was to the lobby when he went to the bar to get his bitter and he didn't see the second unsuccessful

127

applicant for a room, the man who had been sitting in the tan Ford at Mulsey House studying a road map. A thin, thirtyish man with unhealthy-looking spotted pale skin which suggested a late-night indoor life.

The man looked around the lobby and into the bar, from behind the folds of a newspaper he took from his raincoat pocket. He saw Tickell, facing him, or rather facing his newspaper.

Tickell finished his drink and crossed the street on a diagonal to the Bell and Bonnet, which was also black-and-white half-timber but of recent origin, in spite of its deliberately rickety appearance.

Luce, on the brink of taking a fast hot shower, went to her bedroom window to cast a nervous look into the street below. Too bad if Denis walked out of the Imperial right under her nose and vanished elsewhere for the evening.

She saw Tickell. First she felt something jarringly familiar about the man's back, the man in the helmet, and then he turned his head as a bus accelerated toward him and she saw his eye, nose, and mouth. For a moment a dark confusion overtook her. She had gotten up this story for Denis about running away from Tickell, being frightened about what Tickell might do to her, and here he was. Down below.

Coming, very probably, from the Imperial, where her name was on the registry card.

And so was Denis's. Maybe Tickell, as she had, asked if a friend of his named Taunton was staying there.

But how could he know where she was, where Denis was? She watched him opening the pink-curtained brass-scrolled door of the Bell and Bonnet and heard herself whispering, with her forehead against the cold windowpane, "Oh God."

Helmet now under his arm, goggles off, Tickell booked accommodations at the hotel desk, which was painted white with a lacquered design of apple-blossoms. The woman behind the desk was in costume, ruffled white organdy cap and lace-collared, flowered, dimity dress looking back to some indeterminate past. She gave him a doubtful survey and said reedily, "Only a few rooms left, we've the overflow from that . . . *place* across the street. I do have a nice suite though, looking on Queen's Way."

The suite would cost him thirty-five pounds for the night, which of course, she told him, included full English breakfast. Tickell was conducted by a page boy dressed in dark green velvet up a flight of pink-carpeted oak stairs to his suite. His dingy canvas bag was carried with contempt. In his unease, he overtipped the boy and then was left alone among flounces and flowers and gilt, with mirrors to show him how ludicrously out of place the ex-convict John Tickell looked among the cozy splendors of the Bell and Bonnet.

Well. Don't just stand around feeling foolish. He turned off all the lamps the page boy had turned on, seated himself at the window in a butterfly-printed slipper chair, and got out his monocular. He could see into the lobby through the glass door, but not into the bar, where the drawn red curtains made a glow in the deepening evening.

Down at the apple-blossomed desk, the woman in the organdy cap said to herself for the second time in a row, Oh dear, what are we coming to? But the tourist trade had been off this summer and you could, these tight-money days, be just so choosy. She found herself able to provide another suite for the pale young man with the pink spots on his skin.

The sitting room, bedroom, and bath assigned to Ken Yore at thirty-seven pounds a night was called the Petunia Suite. The architects of the hotel had built in fake reconverted attic rooms and the beamed ceilings were at an acute slant. Everything that could be printed with petunias, was. And there were hanging baskets of live petunias and grape ivy at the windows.

Ken Yore looked around him rather hopelessly. Would Betsy spring for thirty-seven pounds along with the rest of his expenses? He hadn't wanted the job anyway. "Following around after somebody? I don't know how to do it, it must be a specialty kind of job."

"Nonsense," Betsy had said. Ken was a cousin of hers, out of work since the police had finally closed the Golden Spell Club in Soho, where he was a croupier. This placed him right at hand,

and she wouldn't have to pay him outlandish money for a simple and perhaps entirely unnecessary few days' work. "All you have to do is keep him in sight and see that he doesn't see you doing it. A twelve-year-old could manage."

"But what kind of suspicious carry-on am I supposed to be on the lookout for?"

Betsy had no intention of filling him in. "Just report in every night for a bit where he goes or doesn't go."

She'd heard Tickell was out of Brixton this week or last. She hadn't seen him since the single prison visit a month after he had been sent there. Whispered unfruitful question, "Have you any idea at all where Al's got himself off to?"

Tickell said that he hadn't, reminding her that her brother was a close one. With a look of trying to be helpful, he murmured that, if he remembered right, once before when eager to depart England in a hurry Al had turned to an old friend who ran a fishing boat out of Falmouth.

With the police still hunting Yore, Betsy had decided not to go poking her nose about Falmouth, tracking down a nameless member of the fishing fleet. In the passage of time, she came to think that that was the way it had happened, though—a sea trip to somewhere, nowhere, a successful escape with plenty of money to live another life under another name in another place. Well, more power to him, not behind bars like Tickell.

Odd though that she had never heard from him,

a safe card or note nobody but she could make head or tail of. At certain times in their lives they had relied heavily upon each other. In the Yore family of eight children, they were the youngest, only a year apart, natural partners against the older horde.

His silence began to bother her a little, then a lot, and all sorts of theories, none of them attractive, began to form in her mind. She tried, often unsuccessfully, to pass them off as mere fancies. And she had her own life to be going on with. There was one very good year, which ended shortly before Tickell got out, during which she was maintained in a delightful flat on St. George's Square in Pimlico by an elderly MP. An unfortunate heart attack canceled this happy arrangement.

Out of money and back on the street, Betsy's thoughts occasionally returned to her brother. Leaving everything else out that he'd taken at Spill—and that was leaving a lot out—there was the fifty thousand pounds worth of gold. And the price of gold these days—!

She was at Gullion's one evening when an old friend named Harry Trevor came over to buy her a drink. They fell into chat and in the course of it Trevor said he'd heard Tickell was out, this week or last. He added in an entirely casual way, "I always wondered, didn't you? About Al?"

"Wondered what?"

"Well, he told me before it happened that he'd be onto a kind of new game with Tick. A new twist, he said. He was quite pleased with himself. So, Tick to jail and Al to . . . where? I wonder if Tick found out about the game."

"You're not saying . . ."

"I'm not saying anything. I just thought it was funny, all along. I wonder where Tick might take himself off to, after he says hello to his friends in town."

The next day Betsy got in touch with her out-of-work cousin Ken. He had started work this morning, after inquiries at Gullion's last night as to Tickell's probable whereabouts. He accompanied Tickell on the Underground to Hammersmith, and then while Tickell was arranging for his motorcycle rented a car at a lot across the Great West Road.

Well, this day's work's over, he told himself, staring at the petunias. I'll just . . . soon . . . call Betsy and tell her where he is.

He was stupefied with the unaccustomed amount of fresh air he had taken in, the effort of keeping the motorcycle in sight, the uncertain ramblings—as at Mulsey House, when it occurred to him that his man might park his cycle and slip out through another gate, or over a wall. Might have seen him following in the Ford, and would now shake him. But, he hadn't. He had led him right here. To this godawful gotten-up ladies' room full of flowers.

Before collapsing thankfully in a chair, he took from his plaid case a bottle of whiskey. If ever he had deserved a drink, it was now. From the bathroom he brought, scowling at it, a glass tumbler painted with flowers and rimmed with gold. He filled it halfway, drank it down, and then called Betsy after finally discovering the telephone under the ruffled skirts of a golden-haired doll.

Betsy congratulated him, although there might not be anything in this trip or any trip Tickell chose to take, but still. "See him into bed before you tuck yourself up, dear. We don't want him wandering off into the night."

Ken had another half glass of whiskey and turned his head to the double bed, canopied in organdy with a great gilt flower catching up the crisp folds at each of the four corners. Just a snatch of shut-eye, until . . .

He hesitated, then with a surly air took off his shoes, stretched out on the bedspread, and went profoundly to sleep.

Luce, in her sense of urgency, broke all her own speed records and did a one-minute shower, whipped on a black jersey dress hung with little golden bells around its low V neck, and rolled and snapped her head as she brushed her hair.

There was only one explanation. Tickell couldn't have landed here by chance. He had followed her here all the way from London. All day. Patiently. Unseen. There were so many motorcyclists they canceled each other out by their very number and a certain sameness about them, their crouch over the handlebars, their boring loony-eyed gear.

Leaving her room, she crossed the hall, went up two doors, and stopped outside 3G. She called Denis's name lightly and when there was no answer put her ear to the door. Silence.

The elevator, dismally groaning, took her down to the lobby. She went into the public bar with the confidence of one entering a natural home-place, and right away saw Denis through a momentary shifting of bodies. He was at a standup table built around a column at the far end. With a tinkling of the little bells at her neck, she joined him.

"I could do with a welcoming gin and lemon," she said, and reached over and brushed his cheek with her fingertips. There was no smile from him, no answering touch of fingers. He went to the bar and came back with her drink.

Leave Tickell's presence here for one, two, three sentences. Get to their own selves first. "Denis, love, for a brainy type you've managed to get everything dead wrong. That silly quarrel—and you dashing off, thinking I'd been waiting all along, maybe marking time, until Tick got out . . . Compared to you, he's nothing to me, absolutely nothing—"

"Nothing is well put," Denis interrupted, red patches on his cheekbones. "You ought to know by now that I do as I please when I please, and do not promise any kind of permanency. Don't you know when you've"—he paused and tried to soften it a bit—"when we've had it?"

Color poured under her creamy skin. Half-enraged, half-pleading, she said, "But look, he's here. Tick's *here*. I saw him not ten minutes ago, and there'd only be one reason. He's following me, or you, or both of us, so let's—"

Denis slammed his empty glass down on the table. "For Christ's sake, Luce, can't you sing another tune?" He turned and walked out of the bar, getting caught up in a group of exiting men loudly singing, "Hello, Dolly."

Luce's following gaze lost him in the busy surge of the lobby and the sudden sharp sting of tears. A man walked to where she stood with her drink in hand, a big red-faced man, and addressed her with a rough kindness and courtesy. "Somebody's in a huff, is that right? And a nice girl like you. My wife's laid up with her bad back, won't leave our room, and I can't stick these pushy bastards . . . will you have a drink with me?"

"Thanks," Luce said. "You couldn't have come along at a better time." When he brought her her new drink, which at his request to the barman was a double, she raised it and said, "Here's to your wife's back."

It was in a way comforting to have a man at her side, a big man at that, with Tickell—inexplicably—somewhere just around a corner. She had never before been afraid of him. She thought she was now, just a little. Or was it Denis who ought to be afraid of Tickell?

Where had Denis gone? Upstairs or out? And was Tickell on his heels right now?

Unable to sit still, she finished her drink in three rapid swallows, thanked her companion, whose name turned out to be Betters, and said she must run.

"That's right," encouraged Betters. "Leave a quarrel long enough and it starts to turn rancid on you."

In the lobby, she cast a quick eye over the shifting knots and circles of people, but Denis wasn't a lobby type. Don't, though, panic—surely he could take care of himself?

Sometimes Tickell carried a knife. "You never know when you're going to have to cut twine about a package, or some such," he had said when she came upon the knife while looking for cigarettes in his coat pocket.

Tick and that temper of his: rare, sudden, awful.

Tickell didn't need his monocular to see Denis walk out the door of the Imperial in what looked like determined and even angry haste. Too good to be true? Maybe. Maybe not. Just out to buy an oddment and return? No—eight or nine doors down the street, he disappeared into a pub whose sign said, "The Whistling Thistle."

He thought the chances were fifty-fifty: that the gold case was with Taunton's other belongings in his room, or on his person. Much better if it was not on his person.

He went to the telephone beside the bed and called the Imperial. "Delivery to make," he said.

"What room's Denis Taunton?" He pulled over his hair a dark blue knitted cap with a couple of fisherman's flies pinned to it, put on his heavily rimmed glasses, and slipped down the stairs and across the street.

Luce was three blocks away and one over, in the other direction from the Whistling Thistle, walking very fast, looking for two men, one following the other, and thinking she must be going a little crazy to be doing this. She had no coat, her arms were bare, and the wind was damp and cold.

Shivering, she would halt momentarily and look into a tobacconist's, a pub, a little corner grocery store.

There had been no answer when she rang Denis's room from the lobby but perhaps he was back by now? She'd catch her death, anyway, if she didn't head back soon.

In the Imperial, neither of the elevators was at the ground floor. Boiling with impatience, she found the door to the service stairs around the corner and ran up to the third floor. His room was just to the right of the stairway. The door of 3G was a half inch or so open.

The most prized of Tickell's experienced and talented keys opened the hotel room door. In seconds, he followed a plan so naturally made he hadn't been aware of thinking it out.

He went in the near-darkness through the

138

bedroom and into the bathroom and opened the window halfway to study a way out other than the door. A grasp of the nearby drainpipe, a projecting roof—probably the hotel kitchen—to the left, just one story down. A side swing and a leap would do it, if the emergency arose. He pulled the shade to the sill.

Then back into the bedroom. Open the door a fraction. The complaining elevators would signal the arrival of anyone returning to the third floor. And the old, hard plastic tiles of the corridor would send along any sound of footsteps.

Use your flash, don't risk even a low-watted hotel lamp. Only one dresser drawer to go through, the rest empty. Raincoat in the closet, nothing in the pockets but an empty cigarette package and a pencil. On the bedside table, a paperback, a folded Michelin map, nothing in the table drawer.

He heard the elevator doors opening and went into the bathroom and listened through a crack. A woman's voice, loud, bleary. "Talk about *me,* you're in no great shape yourself. Don't think I didn't see you smirking away at that Doolittle woman . . ." The voice, and the heavy footsteps of two people, went past the door of 3G.

In the bathroom, Tickell opened the medicine cabinet, finding nothing but a toothbrush, toothpaste, throwaway razor, and a bottle of aspirin. A half-unpacked duffle bag, unzipped, stood on the floor just inside the bathroom door. He bent and fingered through it, touched the cool metal of the case in a side pocket, and was just straightening up holding it in his hand when the bathroom door, pushed inward, hit him lightly in the head as a voice said, "Denis?"

Tickell saw himself with blinding clarity through Luce's shock-widened green eyes. The man who had followed her—followed them—to Catchley. A man who had illegally entered another man's room and was standing in the other man's bathroom. With a gold metal cigarette case in his hand.

With his whole life held in that one hand.

She opened her mouth and before any sound could come out of it he snatched a towel from the rack and bound it over her face. A screaming started under the towel. He flung her forward and heard the silencing whack of her head against the edge of the tub.

He locked the bathroom door. When she came to, here in loverboy's quarters, the explanation, "Tick found me here and knocked me out. He was stealing your cigarette case."

Swearing in his head, and with shuddering regret hampering his hands, he pulled the white towel down around Luce's neck and tightened it. More. Another twist. Hurry. Again, all his strength going into the crossways pull.

Directly below the window, three floors down at the rear of the hotel, was a mountain of dark plastic garbage bags. He lifted and pushed Luce's body (by now it couldn't be anything, Jesus, but a body, could it?) through the half-open window and heard the dull impact as she hit the pile of bags.

He went back into the bedroom, listened at the door, and heard nothing but the sound of music from somewhere up the hall. He closed the door behind him and crossed to the service-stairs' door and went, sagging, knees gone liquid, heart thundering, down the stairs.

Memory, the instant's glance when he had opened the window, showed him Luce's lying-place. The curtains of the kitchen were all pulled, no eyes there to watch a body landing outside. The building extension made one side of a small enclosed courtyard with high brick walls and a gate to the right. The whole arrangement, probably to conceal hotel litter. Beyond it was the windowless concrete wall of what must be a warehouse facing onto the next street. To the far right, at the other end of the hotel, was the car park.

With luck—all right, wild luck—Luce wouldn't be found until, in the morning, some guest looked out a window. Or when the kitchen help came out with another bag of litter.

THIRTEEN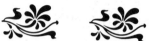

"Oh dear," Flora said, "this tastes like dinners in novels written by Americans describing food in England before the war."

In the immense half-filled dining room of the Haversham, its heavy table linens gleaming and its silverware looking like family antiques, they were served their first nearly inedible dinner in their travels. It consisted of underdone grilled sole apparently basted in water and nothing else; boiled potatoes unyieldingly hard and cold at the center; and what was described as hot salad, which turned out to be slivered cabbage and carrots in a steaming gray dressing of which the main flavor was elderly vegetable oil.

"Thank you, God," Flora said, as the waiter approached with a napkin-wrapped bottle, "here is our wine. I don't suppose they've introduced water or lard into it? Grapes in any form are nourishing."

The waiter, glancing with what seemed like understanding at their full plates, asked, "I hope you're enjoying your dinner?"

Kind Flora said, "It's just that we're not awfully hungry."

"New chef," the waiter said darkly. "There have been complaints. He just started yesterday."

Emily reached for her wine glass and drank with thirst a delicious sauterne. "Two sinking ships will now bob to the surface."

"Bob is well chosen. Bobbish is an English word from way back, isn't it? Sort of a Wodehouse word. You're looking that way tonight, Emily. In spite of the fish. And everything else."

Tired of dimming and modifying herself, tired of hiding, Emily had decided from now on to fly all her flags, and to hell with people thinking she looked happy and enjoying life just because she was mistakenly concluded to be in love. She had put on the attractive supple black Halston with its short swinging skirt and pull-on tank-top, which last night she had backed away from. Her earrings flashed, her perfume gently floated, and close association with wind and damp and roses seemed to have done something irradiating to her skin.

"Thank you," she said. "I think this journey of yours was a healthy idea. Speaking of that, how is your ankle?"

"Asking to be taken to bed," Flora said, taking a sip of black coffee which managed to be at once bitter and weak. "But you mustn't put your

143

candle out yet—I did see that lovely library-lounge affair as we came in.''

The Haversham's library more than paid back for the wretched dinner. It was a nobly tall oak-paneled room with a large fragrant fire, shelf after shelf of real, assembled books and not tattered left-behind paperbacks, comfortable chairs and sofas in conversational islands. At the buffet, with its generous tray of cheeses and silver racks of crackers, a young man in a red jacket amiably dispensed liquors and little cups of powerful espresso. Nine or ten people, standing or sitting, furnished the room with a quietly companionable gaiety.

Emily obtained for herself a cup of espresso, to which the red-coated man, holding a bottle and raising an eyebrow in hospitable questioning, added brandy. She went to the bookcase and found a copy of Colette's *The Blue Lantern,* which she took to a chair near the fire.

She had just gotten to the second page when—as happens unnervingly often to those traveling abroad for a change of scene—someone she knew appeared in the doorway of the library, looked piercingly around for a person or persons who might be talkable-to, and fastened his eyes with astonished and furious recognition on her.

It was Taggard, Ewen Taggard, who had published six books on nature with Faunt and Faunt, all based on his farmhouse life in Vermont and bearing such peaceful titles as, *Newfane Spring, Knee-Deep in Newfane Meadows, When*

Snow Falls on Newfane. These had been selling well and steadily for fifteen years when Taggard, taken by a fit of passion, divorced his wife and married a young Newfane girl. Several months later he sent in a work entitled *Ruminations in a Newfane Barnyard,* devoted to the love-making habits of farm animals and poultry, all of it in execrable blank verse; and illustrated by his new wife with inept childlike crayon drawings. ("Doesn't the sheer innocence of the drawings make you want to cry?" Taggard had written in his letter accompanying the manuscript.)

Emily had no choice but to refuse the book as kindly as possible, adding that she was looking forward to his next volume of prose. With a good deal of thunder and lightning on paper, Taggard wrote back that he was forever finished with Faunt and Faunt, and had a new publisher, and that she, his editor, and his ex-publishing firm, could . . . several explicit barnyard suggestions.

Now he strode across the room and came to a standstill looming over her, all six feet four inches of him. He was a thin ruddy-faced man with an untidy swatch of brown hair and a cowlick which Emily had long thought to be trained in that bucolic fashion.

"Well?" he demanded of her in a stentorian voice. It was hard to tell from just the one syllable, but he sounded as though he had had a good deal to drink. Which was odd, as always when she bought him lunch in New York he made a great audible fuss about being served a glass of cider, preferably cider from Vermont.

"Good evening," Emily said pacifically. "Do sit down." She would have much preferred to make an escape but thought that wouldn't do: highly unprofessional of her.

"I will when I get another . . . when I get myself a brandy." He came back and planted himself on a loveseat at right angles to her chair, leaned forward, and hissed, "I never thought of seeing you or speaking to you again. My *peak* . . ." he took a swallow of brandy. "My *pinnacle*. My *culmination*." His voice was rising and interested eyes turned on him. Heavens, Emily thought, he's sounding a bit indecent.

Another swallow. "And Miss Priss rejects it. Rejects *me*." His face seemed to expand and lengthen with mounting rage. "I won't say anything about my wife's feelings—her talent and innocence spat upon." He put his glass on the table beside him and looked down at the outstretched palms of his large strong hands, as if wondering whether to strangle her with them now or later.

Then he picked up his glass again. "A message from Newfane for you and your bastardly publishers," and threw the rest of the brandy in her face.

The liquid rolled down her forehead, and behind her glasses into her eyes. Through a stinging blur she saw people, motion around her, the red-coated barman, a hard hand on Taggard's arm, but not the barman's arm, Robert's.

Taggard was hauled to his feet, also by Robert. "Who the bloody hell are you?" in Robert's voice.

Emily took off her glasses and found a handkerchief handed down to her, Robert's. As she wiped her eyes and cheeks and blotted her hairline she could see a snippet in some New York column: "Faunt and Faunt editor center of brawl in English bar."

She got up out of her chair and said, "It's all right, he's just . . . I had to turn down a book of his and . . ."

Taggard angrily snatched his arm from Robert's grip. "And who the bloody hell are *you?* The house detective?" He added at shouting volume, "This woman and I were having a private business discussion."

There wasn't time for a long involved explanation, or introduction. And, right now, what was good for the gander was good for the goose: swift and simple.

"My husband," said Emily.

Taggard, rocking slightly on his feet, breathed heavily and glared alternately at both of them.

"I don't think my wife would approve, from a professional point of view," Robert uncannily said, "if I shoved you onto the fire, which is quite handily behind you. Although the idea is tempting."

Looking at his watch, "Shall we go on up to our room, Emily? It's been a long day and it's quieter there—unless you have another angry

147

author lurking at our door?'' He took her hand and they left the library, much to the regret of its other occupants who had been mightily enjoying the scene, or what there was of it before that pleasant-looking man brought it to an abrupt end.

As they went through the lobby, he asked, ''Which room by the way is ours?''

''Mine is on the second floor, the stairs will do,'' Emily said. And on a hasty breath, ''Or do they call it the first floor here, I never can remember.''

Outside her door he paused, looked down at her, put his arms around her, and held her against him, protective and warm. Nice man rescuing her from an ugly encounter, think of it that way. His face in her hair, he laughed softly.

''My poor darling, reeking Emily.''

Speak. And break a silly spell. ''But you do have a room . . .''

''Yes, I was just coming in to the desk when I heard, loud and clear, about your man's peak and pinnacle and came in to investigate.''

''And did you have a nice dinner with Mummy and the third-or-fourth and the BBC?''

''How amazing and delightful to find you—*you,* combative, Emily. Just about ten degrees south of bitchy.'' He laughed again. ''I do believe that one way or another I'm good for you.''

He put his arms elaborately behind his back and bent forward to kiss her mouth lightly. ''Now I will find my room.''

The last man in the kitchen at the Imperial was a young Pakistani who at eleven-thirty had the dubious privilege of seeing that everything in sight was readied for the morning. This meant doing a final swabbing of the counters and stove surfaces, stowing away pots and pans, wet-mopping the floor, and putting out the six heavy bags filled with the residue of the Somerset Hosiers' Association's banquet for seventy. Blinking sleepily, he carried the bags two by two out into the enclosed yard. Someone in the cleaning crew switched on lights in the dining room, which faced the yard but did not see it thanks to heavy interior curtains of dusty-red velvet. But through the center slit in one pair of curtains a streak of light hit a strange object appearing from under a newly tossed bag of garbage. A woman's leg, with nylon on it, and a black sandal on the foot. The leg, the foot, did not move.

The first thing the young man felt was cold terror. The second was personal fear. Whatever it . . . that . . . was, lying under the bag, he might in this strange land be blamed. And imprisoned. For whatever had happened to whatever that was, lying there.

He went back into the kitchen, closed and locked the courtyard door, and left by the opposite door to the staff's parking space, where his bicycle was chained to a post. He pedaled home to his rooming house very fast.

Ken Yore woke at three o'clock in the morning and for a moment looked about him in thick wonderment. He was fully dressed, all the lights were on, these flowers staring at him, what—? Oh, yes. Oh hell. Betsy.

Mentally, he composed his report. "Tickell had a drink or two at a place, a hotel, across the street and I guess dinner, and went up to his room to bed around ten. How do I know he went to bed? He hung out his do-not-disturb sign. And a menu card with what he wanted for breakfast checked." A nice touch, that last; quite convincing. There was a menu card on his own bedside table.

He was too fuddled and sleepy to fill it out and instead had another drink, a short one, undressed, peeled back his ruffle-skirted bedspread, turned off the lights, and went to bed himself.

A screaming from down below, outside, woke Denis at shortly before six o'clock. "Stop that for God's sake, woman!" a man's voice shouted and another man cried, "Don't touch her or move her, the police always say leave them exactly where they lay!"

He got out of bed, went to the window, and put his head out, expecting at the most to behold an inebriate left over from last night, stretched out and sleeping it off.

He saw, in early brilliant sunlight, Luce lying on the dark green plastic billows of bags. Black dress, sun sparkling on the little golden bells, legs oddly twisted but still graceful, head turned to one side at a strange angle, face a peculiar purple in contrast to the whiteness of the bare arms.

There was a milling of people around her, increasing rapidly as three more rushed out of the open kitchen door into the courtyard. The fat woman in an apron gave one final choked-off scream, hand to her mouth. A garbage truck was parked just beyond the open gate. Four bags had evidently been lifted from the pile and lay any which way on the cobblestones.

As, motionless, he watched, hardly aware in his shock what he was actually seeing, he heard the near hooting of a police car. The car drew up beside the garbage truck and two uniformed men got out. There were the inevitable commands to make room, stand back, please.

Over Denis's head and below, to right and left, other windows were flung open and other eyes looked out. Screaming in a different pitch began from a lower-left window. A man above shouted to someone in the room with him, "There's a dead woman out there! At least, she—he's feeling her heart. Now her pulse. He's a policeman. He's shaking his head. So she must be . . . My God, right under our window, right while we were sleeping!"

From the window beside Denis's, a woman's excited voice. ". . . but she was in the bar here last night, I saw her, I remember the dress . . ."

Another car pulled up beside the police car and a white-haired man in tweeds got out. Police doctor, Denis registered, or forensic medicine

151

chap, or whatever they called them. He knelt on the bags and made a swift examination, in the course of which he turned the head with his hands so that the open eyes looked upward.

At Denis.

A police ambulance arrived on the doctor's heels. The body was placed on a stretcher, covered with a blanket, and removed at speed.

But she would always lie there, looking up at him in his window.

The two uniformed policemen remained behind. They now turned in a businesslike fashion to the men and women assembled in the courtyard.

"But look, he's here. Tick's *here*. He's following me, or you, or both of us . . ."

"For Christ's sake, Luce, can't you sing another tune?"

❧ ❧ FOURTEEN

The ringing of the telephone on the bedside table was terrifying.

Denis hesitated. What if it was Flora? It couldn't be. As Leo wasn't in his charge, he hadn't had to call her and say where he was staying.

With his heartbeats sounding in his ears, he picked up the phone. No, he said, wrong room, he wasn't a Mr. Bane.

But he decided then and there not to tell Flora, not to tell any of them about it, about Luce. She would be in the newspapers and perhaps on radio, even television. Flora might or might not see the item. Emily and Marne might, or might not, hear about it. If they did . . .

Oh yes, a girl out in back of the hotel found dead, I didn't want to spoil your day with the story.

Casual everyday violence would be nothing new

to any of them, but when it happened at the hotel your driver was staying in, it would take on a certain reality. There would be a brief presence of death in their midst.

Who was she, Denis, do you know?

No, I have no idea . . .

If Luce was identified as a London girl, would Scotland Yard take over? Wouldn't they zero in on the idea of a man as her killer?

Who, in the last few months, were this woman's close male associates? Whom was she having affairs with?

Well, for one, a chap named Taunton, Denis Taunton. And then of course Tickell.

Should he pick up the phone, put in an anonymous call to the police and tell them to look for a man named Tickell?

Too dangerous—the call would go through the hotel switchboard. Too dangerous right at this time to do anything at all, because his head wasn't working properly. Or was this feeling, entirely new to him, panic?

Just quiet down, make it an ordinary, fine sunny June morning, a day's work ahead, the hotel and Luce soon left behind. Permanently.

Jesus, what was all this sweat about anyway?

He hadn't done anything, anything at all.

Just turned and walked away from involvement rather than heading straight into it. Which—and now he could, he thought, relax a bit—explained the immediate smothering burden of guilt.

Could she, as a matter of fact, have killed

herself, jumped, say, from the roof? No. The idea of Luce killing herself was impossible to hold onto for more than a second. And certainly she would not choose as her bier a mountain of garbage bags.

He found that he was still standing by the telephone. It took an effort of will to move.

In the white robe he had seized when getting out of bed at the screaming, he went into the bathroom. Its window too faced on the back but the shade was pulled to the sill. He was about to turn on the shower when he saw the white towel lying on the tile floor between the end of the tub and the toilet. Why rolled in the center, and why there? He hadn't used a towel last night, coming in around eleven-thirty after the Whistling Thistle closed. He'd just brushed his teeth and fallen into bed.

Would those hours at the pub constitute (not that he ever would need it) an alibi? But then he had no idea when Luce had got it; it could have been one, three, four in the morning. The experts, doing their awful work with the body, would come up with theories about the time of death. And how long it had been since she had eaten her dinner, if she had ever eaten her dinner . . .

His eye moved to the duffle bag sitting near the bathroom door, where he had left it after getting out his toothbrush and toothpaste and razor. An arm of a dark blue jersey tailed out of it and rested on the floor, dejected and lifeless, dead man's arm, but no hand below the cuff. What was wrong about the duffle bag? Something—

Maybe it was the light or lack of it in here thanks to a minimum-watt single bulb supplied by the Imperial, making, with the shade down, a yellow, funereal gloom.

He went to the window and impatiently snapped up the shade. The sunlight struck an object on the sill, caught in a center latch which might in better days here have secured a screen in summer.

It was a little, sparkling golden bell.

For the moment beyond further astonishment or rational thought, he picked up the bell, wiped it with a washcloth and still holding the washcloth dropped it into his robe pocket. He forced himself to look down into the courtyard. The place where her body had lain was plumb-direct under this window.

Finding no sense in this, he dug in his disordered bag on the floor for his cigarette case. There must be some simple, not terrible, explanation. Think it over quietly. If possible.

The case wasn't there. Nerves taking over, he dumped the bag's contents onto the floor: case still implacably missing. Could he have—? He went through all the pockets of his scant wardrobe in vain. He remembered putting it in the bag yesterday morning, because he had every intention of doing a little research of the newspaper files if there was a decent library at whatever town they stopped at for lunch.

He had ably and rewardingly conducted his research.

All right. Granted that Luce had somehow or other gotten into his room for still another scene with him after he had slammed out of the bar and left her there—granted, even if crazily granted, that she had caught Tickell here, searching, and finding what he wanted. And that they had a fight and—

He had brought his Michelin map along with him to the library. After reading all the accounts of the robbery, he had applied himself to a close study of the map. Spill, road names. He hadn't the case with him but he remembered the initials, X, O, E, G. He found on the map the convergence of Xavier, Orme, Enderby, and Gulliver roads.

What (if there was anything but shock and shame and a fleeing from guilt in these musings of his) was so all-important about that crossroads? What matter of, literally, life and death?

Unless it was just plainly and simply the location of the Gadney place. But no, the house according to one newspaper report fronted on Wheatmill Way with a rear entrance on Gulliver Road. He went back into the bedroom and picked up the map. Wheatmill Way curved and then turned sharply south a scale mile or so before the four other roads crossed.

It seemed suddenly like a good idea to get out of here, in a normal and orderly fashion. He took a quick shower, shaved, packed, and after one final and somehow he knew useless search for the cigarette case went down in the elevator to the

157

lobby, half expecting a swarm of impeding police.

But they couldn't, wouldn't detain a whole hotel full of people? Especially with register cards to supply them with names and addresses if wanted. *If* anyone in the Imperial had anything to do with Luce's death.

Was Tickell staying here? In this hotel or nearby? Or had he gone off in the night, mission accomplished?

He made his way quickly to the desk through what seemed to be the same lobby cast of characters left over from last night, all talking their heads off in hushed voices. A coach, no doubt theirs, stood at the curb outside the glass door.

As he paid his bill, the desk clerk, a girl this morning, asked wide-eyed, "Have you heard the awful—"

"Yes. Terrible." He didn't want a rerun, but felt he couldn't afford total incuriosity. "She wasn't staying here, was she?"

"Yes, on the third floor, right near," glancing at his card, *"your very own room.* Fancy that!"

A policeman stood just outside the door. He asked Denis the same questions he must already have asked several dozen times.

"Checking out? Where is your next destination, sir, home, or—?" He added, "Just routine, you understand."

"I'm driving a party of Americans, on a garden tour," Denis said. "I'm not sure, but I'd guess Stourhead this morning." The policeman didn't bother to make a note; his permanent address could be found at the desk. His and several hundreds of others. And after looking into those, there was only the whole town of Catchley to be inquired around, as to who had strangled a girl sometime during the night. The girl identified, from her driver's license in the little satin evening bag she wore gold-clipped to her belt, as Lucetta Panner of 11 Call's Lane, London S.W.

But still feeling himself under some kind of close observation (his own?) Denis walked at a smart but not hurried pace down the street. Normal man eats normal breakfast with normal hunger. He went into a Wimpy's, sat down at the counter, and ordered tomato juice, hot raspberry muffins, and coffee. Even here, several blocks away, Luce was the topic. ". . . makes a change, anyway, from the regular run. A pretty girl, they say. Or was, before whoever . . ." ". . . knifed?" ". . . no, shot, I heard . . ." ". . . no, strangled."

He managed to get down most of his breakfast, paid for it, and left. There was a telephone kiosk ten feet down from the door. He hesitated. No hotel switchboard to worry about now. Call the police? Something like, "The man you want in connection with the Panner girl is named Tickell. He's just out of prison. He was in town last night and may still be here." And then hang up, only a voice, helpful, accurate.

Two considerations, one minor, one major, stopped him.

It was only a patchwork theory of his that

159

Tickell had been found in 3G by Luce, had killed her there and thrown her out of the window. He had no proof whatever that Luce had been correct, that Tickell was actually on the scene.

But if the police did move in on Tickell, rightly or wrongly, and try to take Tickell apart, what was to stop this man from summing up for them the recent vivid history of the dead girl and Denis Taunton? Openly lovers for months, splitting up just about a week ago, the girl running after him from London, finally pinning him down in Catchley—in a bar where he'd in open rejection banged down his drink and left her flat—and shortly afterward meeting her untimely end.

Right below, if they bothered to go back and check, the window of his hotel room.

A chill of sweat broke out on his forehead as he thought about her presence in his room, her fingerprints or palm-print on the corridor doorknob, maybe she'd touched other things, the bathroom door, a table?

If he, in a sense, had Tickell cold, Tickell in a sense had him cold.

For how long? The thought of it, the measuring of it, was intolerable.

There might be another way, a private and personal way, to . . .

A will-o'-the-wisp way. A dangerous way, possibly. But in pondering the alternative wholly worth it.

The man registered at the Bell and Bonnet under

the name of Ernest Dawson would have liked with all his heart and soul to get on his motorcycle and clear away right after it happened. But he'd taken the suite for the night. Funny thing, he could hear the woman in the ruffled headgear at the desk saying to the police (she'd obviously not much liked the look of him anyway as a Bell and Bonnet guest). Funny thing, he took a suite and then he left, bag and all, at . . . what sort of time did you say you think that girl was killed?

Don't consider, right now, what's behind you, but what's ahead of you.

He had a haunted feeling that time was growing short. Even though time had stood still for over four years, at the burned-out house with the well in its forgotten garden.

Make arrangements, plans, get about the task, get it done. Go back to London and—

Could he go back to London? Would the police, in the morning, arrive at Luce's flat, looking for someone or something to offer a lead to her killer? His clothes were there, but out of long habit were mute as to the identity of their owner: no labels, no personal papers carelessly carried in pockets.

Sooner or later they might get around to where she worked, Gullion's, talk to people, get a picture of Luce and her life and her man . . .

Her men. John Tickell and Denis Taunton. A great freeing wave swept away some of his tension.

In the first place, there was nothing to connect

a man in a dark blue fisherman's cap, a man named Ernest Dawson staying expensively at the Bell and Bonnet, with a man named Tickell who currently lived with Luce. Get that through his head.

In the second place, even if they on a five-hundred-to-one chance put the two names together into one person, there was another man, staying right in the same hotel, right down the hall, another man who had recently lived with Luce.

In a strange moment of cold objectivity, Tickell nodded his head. Yes. Taunton could look highly promising, to the police.

Scrub London. Lie low here until check-out time and think. Spill oughtn't to be too far from Catchley. Why make a journey into danger and then another journey down again, to the southwest of London, to Somerset?

He'd need a wheeled hauling box to fasten at the back of the motorcycle. To hold that heavy weight and bulk of gold thrown down on top of Yore's body. He'd need rope, and climbing boots, and—Now at five o'clock in the morning, he made a list of what he'd need, on the Bell and Bonnet's stationery.

Betsy Yore was waked at the rude hour of nine-thirty by the ringing of her telephone. Accustomed to sleeping until at least eleven, she answered crossly, "Yes, what the . . . what is it?"

Ken Yore told her what it was. The murder of

Luce, and then, "Unless there's some kind of game on, she was tracking him in her car and taking care to stay out of his sight."

After a pause, Betsy said, "I can't somehow seem to be able to take it in. *Dead*—you're sure?"

Yes, Ken was sure. "I'm heading back as of now," he said. "If you think I'm going to go on following on the heels of someone who . . . probably . . ."

"Wait a second. Let me think. Is he still there?"

"I suppose so, I don't know. I'm calling from the booth in the lobby. I've been down here since seven. No sign of him. There's no one named Tickell registered here, but I saw him check in at the desk and go up the stairs last night." He went on, remembering his dereliction from duty just in time, with his tale of Tickell going early to bed.

"Well then, he's in the clear, isn't he?" Betsy asked in bewilderment.

"Unless he did it before that, no one seems to know yet when at night it happened."

"What's check-out time there?"

"Twelve noon. But I told you I'm leaving right now."

"Look, Ken, there are things I know about you that I wouldn't like to pass along to interested parties. You stay put right there. After all, no one can do anything to you in a hotel lobby. One way or another I'll call you back there in a bit. I'm all in a muddle, I have to think."

"But if he leaves earlier—"

163

"If he leaves earlier, you know what to do. I just told you what to do. I'll stay in all day. Waiting to hear from you, about how your job's going."

Over three cups of coffee, Betsy tried to marshal her thoughts and make them add up to some sort of conclusion.

Tickell was living at Luce's, according to Ken. A bar girl at Gullion's, very well spoken of, again according to Ken.

Off went Tickell to a place named Catchley. On his way to somewhere? Wait a minute, get out the road map for the southwestern counties. (Her amiable MP had bought her a nice yellow Rover, which she had since sold, but she still had her road maps in an old shoebox.)

The town of Spill was, if she was reading the map scale right, thirty-five or forty miles away from Catchley.

Luce, Tickell's girl, follows him to Catchley. Why? Scenting profit of some kind? Hidden gold and other alluring things?

Whether secretly meeting or pursuing her lover, Luce gets herself killed.

No, she couldn't leave all this in Ken's unwilling and inefficient hands. And the fewer people who knew about it the better, when and if it came to . . .

There was only one thing to do. Find out about it in person, face to face, if there was anything to find out about.

At ten-thirty, dressed and ready, she called Ken back at the Bell and Bonnet, asking the operator for the number of the phone booth in the lobby.

"Any sign of our friend?"

"No, and I'm just about going crazy sitting on my hands here."

"Okay, forget it," Betsy said. "I can't stay in after all, a friend's invited me for a few days to Whitstable. I'll settle up what I owe you when I get back."

She went out and rented a car, a dark green Subaru. Spill was a long chance, probably nothing whatever going on at Spill except the cows having another chew of grass and clover. But she was by nature a taker of long chances, and told herself that a day or so in the country never hurt anybody.

FIFTEEN

Robert's room at the Haversham was next to Flora's and he was treated to the unfamiliar pleasures of the very early morning when Leo began a campaign of barking. "A mouse, I think," Flora apologized later. "He woke me too." After several unsuccessful attempts to go back to sleep, he groaned and got out of bed.

When he went downstairs at six, the dining room had not yet opened and the elderly clerk at the desk was gently nodding, with an occasional backward jerk of his shoulders and snapping open of his eyes. The morning outside was fresh and brilliant. There was nothing to do but accept its invitation and go strolling in search of coffee.

The High Street, with its expensive shops, its country inns embellished with climbing roses, its several French restaurants, looked soundly and sensibly asleep. He turned into Queen's Way and was pausing in doubt before a grimy cafe which called itself "Le Twenty-Four Hours." Some patron had evidently lost his dinner, or midnight feast, near the doorstep. It seemed a good idea to press on, no matter how urgent the desire for coffee.

In the near distance, he heard a woman screaming. An abiding curiosity about everyone and everything was a part of his nature. He began to walk along the sidewalk toward the unruly and uncivilized sound. After a block or so, a police car hooted past him. The car turned, a block up ahead, into the parking space beside a hotel named the Imperial.

Instinctively his hand moved at his side. Of course his camera was there, slung by its strap over his right shoulder. It was as normal an item of daily dress as his shoes. A police ambulance went by as he walked up the street. It too turned in beside the Imperial.

He entered the parking space and without furtiveness but with caution walked between cars until from beside one of them he could get a clear view through the wide-open gate into the enclosed courtyard of the hotel, where there was a bustle of motion and voices but no more of the screaming.

He saw the girl in the black dress sprawled on the pile of garbage bags. He raised his camera. Professionally speaking, too good (humanly speaking, too frightful) to be true, to be really happening here in a quiet English village on a delightful sunny morning.

The purpled face . . . now where . . . when . . . ?

His camera recorded the doctor's arrival and examination of the body, the police photographers busy with their own cameras, the measurement-taking, all the procedures attendant upon sudden death. Then the lifting of the body onto the stretcher, a crisper view of the girl before the blanket was whipped over her.

What was this crime, now reposing on film inside the Canon? And what was nagging at his memory, somewhere deep under the surface of shock and pity? The swing of bobbed, black, silk hair, the sun gleaming on it when the doctor had moved her head with his hands . . . the face was purple, dreadful, dead, but the hair was glistening with life.

Then he remembered, and saw a mental photograph. Yesterday morning in Pym, a car stopping beside the herringbone brick sidewalk under the hawthorn tree. A girl's voice, "Can you direct me to the Horsecollar?" The short black hair spilling across her cheek as she leaned toward him. On the same film clip, Flora's voice said, after the car had pulled away, "That's where Denis is staying."

Well . . . so what?

The dining room of this hotel might now be open and he felt a strong need for coffee, lots of it. He went around to the front and in at the glass door, where a policeman stood. Without pausing to think about it, he went to the desk and asked if Denis Taunton was a guest at the hotel.

The girl flicked through register cards in a file

on the counter. She said, "Yes," adding with a grin, "but I don't know if at this hour he'd thank you for . . ." and switching directions, "I suppose you've heard about the *awful* . . ."

"Yes," Robert said. "Is the dining room open?"

"No, not till seven, but there's a place round the corner to your left that opens at five."

Drinking his coffee, he told himself that he was the wrong sex and in the wrong century to be having what might be described as an attack of the vapors. Perhaps it had something to do with the sight, when he had left the car at Hardings Lacey for a breath of fresh air, of Denis leaning over Emily in the little summerhouse, wrapping her in his jacket, lending her warmth. And why not? An attractive woman, an American, unattached, obviously solvent.

He reminded himself for a second time that at the moment he was not entitled to any kind of possessive anger about Emily, or in a position to censor Emily's men. If Denis Taunton was in the process, here and now, of becoming one of them.

But it would be interesting, when the press took off on the death of the girl behind the Imperial Hotel, to see who she was, and where she had come from, and what fatal pursuit of business or pleasure had taken her from Pym to Catchley.

When Denis came into the lounge of the Haversham on the exact tick of nine o'clock, he found Flora and Leo waiting for him in the sunny little writing room off the main lobby.

As usual, the reservations for the coming night were to be made before their departure in the car. "Good morning, Denis," Flora said. "You're looking marvelously wide-awake. I'm just about ready for an afternoon nap. After Stourhead, Buscot Park, I think. It's quite near Oxford. I thought we'd stay at the Danforth in Oxford."

Denis bent to quell the leaping, adoring Leo dancing about his trouser legs.

"I think a slight change of plans is called for. Down, Leo! There's something just not quite right about the left-front wheel bearing. I won't bore you with the mechanical details." Emily now joining them smiled to herself; familiar kind of male phraseology.

"Oh dear," from Flora, "we aren't stuck here? Not that it isn't—"

"No, we'll get easily through a day's driving. But I've been on the phone to Gold Star, the car can't be trusted with just any garage. There's one in a town called Spill which specializes in foreign makes and collectors' items, and that's where we should head at the end of the day."

His researches at the library had been thorough. He added, "I don't know if it's on your list but I'm told there's a very beautiful garden—Georgian house—the works—Glastondel, near Spill. I shouldn't think you'd want to miss it."

"Oh, of course, Glastondel. We can do Buscot Park the next day. How delightful to be forced off course when it's to Glastondel. I'd lost my page of notes on it, and but for the grace of God or you or the wheel, would have missed it."

From somewhere close behind her Emily felt before she saw the presence of Robert, who must have just come in from outside the hotel because a freshness of light and air seemed to breathe from his very clothing.

"Are we," Flora asked wistfully, "to leave you here to continue finding camera angles and moving rocks at Mulsey House?"

Robert was brisk. "Not at all. As my doomed gardener is forced to go from place to place to escape unwelcome passion, I'm going to have to collect gardens anyway, and I'd prefer to do it in your company if I'm not in the way."

He gave Emily a sideways glance. "You're looking doubtful. I'll be more than happy to share expenses while I'm with you."

Emily had been looking doubtful because of the, to her, loaded phrase, "to escape unwelcome passion," but then remembered that she had decided to put all that nonsense behind her.

She had for some reason slept extraordinarily well, and in fear of encountering Ewen Taggard, at the ready with more abuse, in the dining room, had had a pleasant lazy breakfast in her room. She had put on a suit, light as powder, of heliotrope Irish tweed and an easy open-throated ivory silk shirt, and without exactly being aware of it presented an appearance of freshly minted charm.

"I have no objection," she said to Robert,

"provided you don't snatch my back seat from me to take over your new-found friend."

The Haversham was not a believer in despoiling its old and beautiful bedrooms and main rooms with radio or television sets. To an intently listening ear, there was only one news-bearing voice as the four of them went out through the lobby to the car. It came from a distant corner, a very old woman talking loudly to a very old man.

". . . *quite* dead, they said. A young gel. In some sort of cocktail getup, perhaps coming home from a party, and then . . ."

And Flora's early morning walk with Leo, after a tour of the lawns and gardens behind the hotel, had taken her up the sedate High Street, where at the far end she found a French bakery and gourmet shop open. There, the talk with the counter attendant was not of death but of Strasbourg pâté, blanched asparagus, Parma ham, and would these white grapes be sweet? or perhaps the Israeli melon . . .

Robert had no desire to place an instant dark smear over everybody's morning. But at ten o'clock, when news might reasonably be expected on the car radio, he could contain himself no longer and reaching forward flicked it on.

". . . which is felt will have serious repercussions throughout the Common Market," said a woman just concluding the lead story. She went on to a train wreck in Scotland, a fire at the bathing pavilions at Blackpool, a riot in Notting

Hill in which seven rioters and six policemen had been severely injured.

"Oh dear," Flora said in mild protest. "And on such a nice morning, Robert."

"I need just one news fix a day," Robert said, talking through the weather report for the southwestern counties. "And then I promise you silence."

"The Mayor of Sparkwich goes on trial today for alleged borrowings from the town treasury. And, a late news bulletin, the body of a girl strangled to death was found early this morning in the rear courtyard of the Imperial Hotel in Catchley."

Denis reached out an instinctive hand to the radio switch and in that fraction of a second Robert turned and looked at him with one eyebrow just slightly raised, the eyebrow with the thin scar cutting through it. Denis put the hand back on the wheel. It was only a flash, a flicker, the exchange of glances, but Denis thought, Here we go. And this is only the beginning.

". . . identified as Lucetta Panner of Call's Lane, London. On a cheerier note, the tenth annual dog show at . . ."

Robert turned off the radio. "I will not inflict you with dog shows," he said, smiling over his shoulder at Flora.

"But much nicer than murders," Flora said. "I'd almost think I was back in New York. And in Catchley of all places. I'm glad we've left it behind us."

And that, miraculously, was all. For the moment.

But, not having Leo with him for the night, he had not been obliged to call Flora and tell her where he and her poodle were bedding down.

So that, to the other occupants of the Gaspard, he and the Imperial Hotel were unconnected.

Robert opened his mouth and then closed it.

He found himself deeply disturbed by the other man's total lack of response of any kind —surprise, shock, or, "Oh yes, everybody in the hotel was talking about it." And yet he had been staying at the Imperial. Could he have checked out before the body was discovered and the commotion started? Why, at least, hadn't he, if it came as news to him, said the natural, the obvious, the inevitable thing, that that hotel was where he had been staying last night?

He turned his head and looked at the silent, handsome profile. He didn't know Denis well enough to read the planes of his face and the set of his muscles. The large hands were steady on the wheel. The blue eyes were firmly on the road. The Gaspard went smoothly and softly on, floating up and down the long low chalk hills.

He thought it wise at the moment to keep his musings to himself, instead of asking a simple open question of their driver. He had a sudden mad vision, if he did ask the question, any question about the dead girl, of Denis holding them all hostage. Or starting a runaway dash from the police at a hundred miles an hour with

174

his passengers hanging for dear life onto the braided silk wall straps.

But, and better sooner than later, several phone calls seemed to be the sensible course.

Reading from her notes at a little after eleven, Flora's voice broke what had been on her part a sleepy silence. Denis at his wheel was never given to a spate of talk, having a very low threshold himself for listening to idle chatter. Robert and Emily had exchanged a few comments on this church or that hill and what particular cows those might be to the right under the sycamore trees, Friesians perhaps?

On and off, Emily thought, "My wife." And, "My husband." Both of them saving the trouble of long-winded explanations and qualifications.

" 'The gardens at Stourhead,' " recited Flora, " 'are among the finest in Europe. They were laid out by the London banker Henry Hoare, in the middle of the eighteenth century and were inspired by classic literature and the landscape paintings of Claude Lorraine. Henry Flitcroft designed the temples surrounding the lake and these contain sculptures by . . .' "

She broke off and said, "I have the strangest feeling —how to describe it?—of *explosiveness* in this car. As though there were a lot more people here than the quiet four of us. Oh well, I suppose it's just being up so early, and Emily and I hardly touched our dinners last night, the food was so . . . in about half an hour, Denis, let's stop and

175

get the hamper out."

"And if you can find a scenic spot that's not far from a public telephone I will be much obliged," Robert amended.

While Flora passed around warmed croissants with pâté to spread upon them—("Emily, if you'll cut melon and fold ham around it, and Denis, perhaps the Moselle?")—Robert walked fifty yards to a telephone kiosk under an apple tree at the roadside. First he called the Imperial, identifying himself as a reporter from the Bath *Chronicle,* and asked the desk at exactly what hour the girl's body had been found. At ten to six, the girl said, give or take a minute or so. Was there, she inquired eagerly, anything else he wanted to know?

Yes, there was: When had Denis Taunton checked out? But he could not, because the question in its context might be passed along to the police. He had, however, obviously been still in his room when Robert had stopped at the desk at close to six-thirty. The same girl, from the voice, grinning at him and saying, "I don't know if at this hour he'd thank you for . . ."

"Two more things. When do you come on, at the desk, and is there any kind of unguarded back way out of the hotel?"

"I'm, help me God, here at five every morning. And there's no back way because we've had people skip off in the last year or so and everything's locked up tight, you can only go out through the lobby. The police checked anyway

—nothing broken or forced."

His next call was to the Horsecollar in Pym. A man with a surly voice answered. "I've got my hands full and all, can't you ring back later?" No, said Robert, he couldn't.

"Wait a minute then . . . yes, Taunton stayed here Saturday night and left in the morning."

"Did he, do you know, have any visitors? I'm trying to contact a mutual friend, a girl . . ."

"I've no idea, mate. The only one who might know is Ida. I'm mostly on the bar unless I'm press-ganged to the desk like this morning. She's off today. No phone, but if you want her address . . ." His hand holding the receiver beginning to ache with tense frustration, Robert said thanks, no.

Probably fantasy, all of it. But now there seemed, in this fantasy, a second reason for staying firmly, invited or uninvited, with the garden tour in the Gaspard.

"You're out of luck, Leo," Flora said, looking again at her Stourhead notes. " 'Dogs in gardens October to end of February only.' But if Denis takes you for a walk you can listen to the birds—they're supposed to have the loveliest birds here."

The three strolled the Sand Walk, silenced by the magic of the view down and across the main lake. Emily wondered what was wrong with her to bring a feeling close to tears, at sheets of blue-bells spilling under heroic trees, at towering rhododendrons pink and pearl and silver-mauve.

Flora turned to Robert and said in a manner touchingly shy, "As you have your camera with you, would it be too much to ask . . ." She hesitated. "Or too corny, do you think? That's the Temple of Flora over there on the other side, and I thought Reg . . . my husband, you know . . . might be pleased if—"

"Of course," Robert said, glancing to see how many exposures he had left after his morning session in the courtyard.

"I'll wander a bit, I want to see the Pantheon and find the sweet chestnuts and the white willows, whatever they are." Emily drifted away from them.

At the temple, they waited while a queue of children wearing summer camp shorts-and-shirt uniform left in an orderly fashion while their young woman in charge cried, "The tulip trees! How many of us can identify a tulip tree?"

Robert looked his setting over. "I think among the columns. You're dressed for them." Flora wore an expensive and shapeless garment of cream silk pleated from shoulder to hem, and a large fringed triangular scarf to match. Her straw hat was droop-brimmed and wreathed in yellow roses. The most tactful adjective for her comfortable laced-up brown shoes was sturdy.

"If you could just manage to miss the shoes?" she requested. "Reg laughs at my walking shoes. But then, they're not his feet."

During the taking of half a dozen pictures in

different plays of light and shadow, several portrait shots as well as three-quarter length omitting the shoes, they had a short conversational exchange.

"How much if anything do you know about Denis?"

"Well that, first of all, he was recommended as their best driver by the car-rental place. That he's pleasant to be with, well-mannered, a gentleman if that isn't too old-fashioned a word. Why"—suddenly—"do you ask?"

It wouldn't do to say why. Instead, Robert murmured to his camera, "He seems rather taken with Emily."

"Is he? But is that so odd? She's in her own quiet way one of the most attractive people I've ever known. However, she's, in another old-fashioned phrase, already spoken for. Although . . ."

Robert took his last shot. "Although what?"

Flora gazed at him with her natural unselfconsciousness, his face and eyes and hair, his hands, his easy grace of carriage.

"Although I really do think . . ." She stopped abruptly, hearing the thought she had been keeping to herself floating now, almost spoken, through the sunlit columns.

"So do I," said Robert. "Shall we take a swing around to the Pantheon? Duly observing the tulip trees as we go."

SIXTEEN

The somber moving mountains of purple-blue storm clouds to the west, the mighty theater lighting of tremendous shafts of gold striking a cottage here, a green rounded hilltop there, brought only one reaction from Betsy Yore as she drove into the town of Spill at a little after five o'clock.

My God, did I remember to bring my umbrella?

She had no specific schedule to follow upon her arrival. She would follow her nose, or her instincts, as she did every day of her life.

The first obvious project was to find a place to stay for the night, preferably a place where Tickell might also be staying. She stopped at a little pub near a farm on the outskirts of the town and over her gin and lemon asked a fat friendly girl at the bar what sort of accommodations were available in Spill.

The girl gave her the names of places and street

addresses, four of them. "Now if you're here to see Glastondel, so many people are, there's the Aves Inn, where they have . . ." Betsy waved aside any detailed descriptions. She wanted to see for herself; a feeling in her bones would be needed to indicate exactly the sort of place a Tickell might choose. Not that she knew him all that well, a few drinks on and off with him and Al, and no professional services on her part involved. And then, of course, that long night in her flat, with the Gadneys' gardener, Arthur Kemp.

The Aves Inn was well beyond the far side of town, might as well get that over first. She drove along Xavier Road, past farms and woodland, and turned north on Lord's Lane, which wound for about half a mile. An immense clipped yew hedge to her left ran for a good part of this distance. That tourist attraction, she supposed, whatever its name was, she had forgotten. Left again past more of the clipped yew, into Bottomly Road. The Aves Inn was across the road from where the hedge came to an end, its own corner-turning edging the property marked by a marble column topped with an urn.

The inn was rambling, white, with a thatched roof, fruit trees trained against its walls, four or five blue doors, a garden full of flowers of which the only ones Betsy could identify were roses, an entrance arch of lacy white-painted wrought iron at the brick pathway leading to the main blue door, and path hedges of some lavender-colored thing that smelled sharply—of all things—of

181

lavender. Betsy took a comprehensive look and said to herself, "Never."

Next on her list was a guest house, an ugly square newish brick house with a sign on the balding front lawn, "Guests, Moderate." A small boy and girl were roller-skating in the driveway and a woman could be seen at the back of the house taking washing off a line in haste, her eye on the purple clouds now overhead.

Not Tickell's kind of thing, Betsy thought, in case Tickell was up to something ordinary people might not be up to—whatever it was. Eyes to note his comings and goings; and their paying guests must form a subject for family conversation.

Another little inn, called the Tit-for-Tat, smothered in climbing roses, with a sign hung by a chain on its door, "Sorry, Fully Occupied." Was it fully occupied because Tickell had taken the last remaining room? As she watched from the car, two large tweedy women came around from behind the inn, both holding on leashes enormous formidable looking dogs, an elkhound and an outsize boxer. If I were him, Betsy thought, I wouldn't fancy the idea of dogs getting up an interest in my scent. The Tit-for-Tat must have kennel accommodations; surely a tiny place like this wouldn't be able to contain such animals.

Her final hostelry was on the High Street across the road from the railway station. As she approached it, a car going in the opposite direction caught her eye—a, in Betsy's adjective, drop-dead car, not purple but close to it, cream top, four people in it, made her late MP's black Rolls look like an upstart. Perhaps it was going home to its garage in—what was the name of that place with the yew hedges?—yes, Glastondel.

The Spill Arms looked to her just right for Tickell, a commercial hotel, sooty brick, large, stingy-windowed, showy fake marble pillars at the entrance with the paint peeling off them at the tops, no canopy, no doorman. The lobby was narrow and unadorned except for a dusty brocade sofa which looked hard as rock, a chair to match, and a potted palm turning brown at the tips of its fronds. A sour-faced gray-haired woman knitting a sock sat in the chair.

She went to the desk where a thin man smelling of gin presided, and said she wanted a room for the night, preferably on the front. "Okay, nice view of the railway tracks," he said, eyeing her in a way she was well used to. He'd probably be knocking at her door at midnight to try his luck.

She signed the register Elizabeth Kennett, using her mother's maiden name. Tickell probably wouldn't show, and this was all probably codwallop, but you never knew.

Her room was just about what she'd expected, small, with twin beds covered in rose-colored chenille spreads very close to being exhausted by laundering, bright brown varnished chest of drawers and bedside table, dingy pink armchair, closet with a mirror hung slightly crooked on the door and a few bent old wire hangers on the rod inside.

Not having wanted to make her inquiry in the hearing of the knitting woman in the lobby, Betsy went to the phone and called the desk. "Has a man named Tickell, John Tickell, checked in?" she asked. And in case the clerk might pass along to Tickell that a you-know-what-looking blond had been asking for him, she added, "Our Pen Pals Society is meeting here, and so far we don't know what each other looks like."

The last thing Tickell would connect her with was a pen pals society. But then, he hadn't used his own name at the Bell and Bonnet and probably wouldn't use it here, right on the scene so to say.

She was not surprised to find that there was no Tickell registered at the Spill Arms. But now, toward the end of the day, people, any kind of people, were thinking about eating and drinking. He would probably not choose the hotel dining room, which she had seen through glass-paned doors in the lobby; or would he? Anonymous people in an anonymous hotel. If he chose a pub instead, it would be likely to be nearby; he wouldn't want to be broadcasting his presence in wide-ranging display in the town of Spill.

It was only five twenty-five; time for a spot of gin from her flask while she thought things over.

In his bathroom on the floor below, Tickell was cosmetically occupied. Carefully following the directions on the label of Change-'n'-Glow Hair Magic, he washed his hair in the basin, mixed the Hair Magic half-and-half with 20-volume

184

peroxide, and toothbrushed it into his hair, beginning at the side parting. The color he had chosen was Russian Sable, but the bottle label picture showed a perfectly ordinary brown, not light, not dark. Just brown. He left the dye on for twenty-five minutes which he thought would never end. Then he stepped into the shower and washed his hair twice with hotel cake soap. At the first washing, the dye ran into his eyes and stung them.

He dried his hair and the rest of him. He looked at himself with some distaste in the mirror. Eye whites an irritated pink, hair nothing-brown instead of sterling silver. He asked himself, Who, now, in the hell am I?

The hair wouldn't have mattered if the job could have been done by night. But it was too complicated for that. The willow trees in daytime would conceal him and his activities from any passers-by on the road. But by night, there would be the betraying pierce of a pencil flash as he went about his business, knotting the rope around the tree, and then . . .

He did not admit to himself that death, even four-year-old death, at the bottom of the well was something not to be encountered at night.

He had worn his helmet while registering in the lobby and when he was ready to go downstairs a glance from the desk clerk would be nothing to worry about, a glance at a brown-haired man in a neat dark green suit. Might as well eat in the hotel dining room, he thought; like any ordinary traveling man who would put up at the Spill Arms.

As the elevator doors closed behind him in the lobby, Betsy Yore, who had been sitting on the rocky sofa, said in a voice of bright amazement, "Why, *Tick,* of all people! Who'd ever believe it?"

He stopped where he stood. Or was it his heart stopping?

She got up and came over to him, looking much the same as he remembered her, perhaps a little battered but the skin fresh with makeup, the chrysanthemum hair fair and springing, the blue eyes sparkling under double sets of glossy brown false eyelashes.

She put out a hand and he had no choice but to take it. Merrily, chattily, she went on, watched and listened to by four other people, sitting and standing, and the desk clerk.

"What a piece of luck, when I thought I was stranded alone in this"—an eye on the clerk, she lowered her voice—"well, hardly Claridge's, right? You know me, not the shy type, how would you like to treat me to drinks and dinner? We can have a good old talk about the old times."

Tickell found saying anything at all extremely difficult as something had happened to his throat muscles. No swift excuse, no alternate engagement came even remotely to mind.

"Well, I . . . I thought I'd just eat here in the dining room, it's been a long day and . . ."

She took his arm firmly and headed them toward the doors of the dining room. Lowering

186

her voice again, she said, "Sometimes these crummy places have good food—people traveling on expenses like to treat themselves to at least a decent meal after selling biscuits or ladies' undergarments all day."

She felt the trembling of the arm under the dark green sleeve. She had a heady sense of triumph.

Tremble on, Tick.

To the headwaiter, she said, "A corner table, please," and to Tickell, "We'll have lots to talk about after all this time, won't we? Might as well be able to hear ourselves."

The room was about three-quarters filled, fashionable late dining not being the custom at the Spill Arms, and there was a clatter and chatter of voices all around them.

Betsy's openly inviting looks produced a waiter at their corner table immediately. "A champagne cocktail," she said. "Or, as I'm thirsty and you look rushed, dear, bring me two. No, make it three."

"A double gin and lemon," Tickell said.

Lots to talk about . . . ?

There was a next to impossible question he must ask: the perfectly normal question. So, impossible not to ask it.

"What are you doing here . . . client business far from home?"

"Good old Spill, funny coincidence, isn't it. I'm on my way to Penzance to spend a few days with a friend. He has a nice little cottage by the sea. And you can stand just so many hours on trains and buses, so I thought I'd stop off and get my beauty sleep here.''

The tray of drinks arrived. She took a deep relishing gulp of her first champagne cocktail. ''I've developed a taste for these. Very thinning, as drinks go.''

Very expensive, as drinks go.

Elbows on the table, hands cupping her glass, she leaned toward him and Tickell fought an impulse to lean back, far back. He could feel the sweat on his forehead and upper lip. ''Hot in here,'' he explained.

''Now let's see, what's different about you? Oh, your hair. I liked the gray, you know, I thought it was distinguished. Particularly with a youngish sort of face.''

He reached for his drink and then drew back his hand, because it was shaking. ''Well, these days people add ten years onto your age when they see gray hair. And with jobs so . . .''

Christ, the next thing she'd ask was, what was his job?

''You're working, then? Pretty quick, I'd say, you just out of Brixton.''

''Yes—peddling motorbikes.''

''Really?'' Eyes wide with interest. ''Two of my brothers are out of a job. Any hope for one or both of them at your place?''

''No, they're letting chaps go who don't meet quotas, I've got to scurry to meet mine, I'll tell you that.''

''You've got to scurry . . . poor Tick.'' She

finished her first cocktail and started on her second. "Oh God, here come ten more people, we'd better order now or we'll be waiting all night."

At her lifted hand, their waiter came back. He stood watching the sweep of her false eyelashes under a shimmer of pale blue eye shadow as she studied the menu.

"Mmmm. The potted shrimp to start with. The steak with Béarnaise sauce, asparagus with Hollandaise, the endive and anchovy salad, and the apricot cream tart. My friend will see to the wine order."

Tickell, intent on his own card to escape for a few moments the terrible, close, sparkling gaze, saw that she had ordered the most expensive food available in each category.

Was he being deliberately taunted, threatened, challenged? Blackmailed by menu?

Or was she just used to men buying her anything at all she wanted, along with buying the use of her body?

Again, he found it hard to move his lips, to speak. "A cup of tomato soup, the fried haddock and . . . green beans, no salad, no dessert."

"You're forgetting the wine," Betsy said. She lifted her eyes to the waiter's. "Something delicious and, I think red, to go with my steak. Suppose we leave it to you."

Then she turned, smiling, back to her companion. "Here I am on my last cocktail and you haven't even touched your drink. Are you trying to show me you're a reformed man? A born-again something-or-other?''

She felt a savage excitement. Teasing him this way, or could it be called torturing him? Playing with fire and enjoying it. That girl, Luce, dead as of some time last night. She had been staying at a hotel too, and he hadn't even been at the same hotel but at one across the street from it.

Of course, she couldn't know whether he had had anything to do with the murder. And his shattered state, the trembling of the arm, and the hand which was afraid to pick up a drink, *might* be the result of the years in prison and then being sprung and now having to fight for a living selling motorbikes.

But she didn't think so.

Excitement shoved aside hard common sense. She had to know.

''Have you, one way or another, ever heard from Al? Under some other name from shall we say some faraway place?''

Some faraway place like a grave, unmarked. Maybe.

''No,'' Tickell said. ''No, I haven't.'' Don't embroider, don't expand, don't say, He was the lucky one that got away. Just leave it.

Betsy waited while her dish of potted shrimp on lettuce was placed before her, and Tickell's cup of tomato soup served. ''The wine right away?'' the waiter asked her, ignoring the man who would no doubt pick up the check.

''Yes, oh, lovely.''

190

Through a sort of blur Tickell saw the label on the wine bottle, in French, scrolled lettering, probably costing the earth. Betsy took a trial sip. "Delicious." The waiter, resisting an impulse to pat her shoulder, left them.

"Well, but about Al," Betsy said, after a mouthful of shrimp. "He's in touch with me off and on. South America, I won't say exactly where. I'm not a queen of morals myself, but I can't say I approve of his line of business—what's the matter, Tick?"

Tickell choked on a spoonful of soup and held his napkin to his face. "Pardon me," he said. He went at speed to the rest rooms, just barely making it before throwing up. Then he washed his face, but there was no way to wash the red from his eyes.

How could he possibly go back to that table and that woman?

He had to.

He stopped in the bar on the other side of the lobby and had a fast double brandy. And then, after a few minutes of slow deep breathing, a single. Let her gobble her steak and swill her wine.

Now, steadied and a little drunk, he rejoined her. He was greeted with sympathy. "Poor thing, an attack of the collywobbles?"

He managed a few bites of his haddock and a forkful of green beans. Over her apricot cream tart and coffee, Betsy glanced at her watch.

"Awful to eat and run, but I've got to be up

early to catch my train. My friend's picking me up in his car at Plymouth. Don't rush your coffee, you just sit and enjoy yourself. And I'll say thank you, good night, and good-bye, Tick, see you around in London I hope." She got up and left the table.

At the desk, she stopped and picked up a railway timetable. She went up to her room, closed the self-locking door, and remembering that thieves are good at locks wedged a straight-backed chair under the doorknob.

But he'd hardly kill two girls in a row, would he? *If* he'd done that Panner girl.

She was glad, though, that she had thought to bring along in her large leather handbag her black Beretta automatic pistol.

✿ ✿ SEVENTEEN

"Delightful!" Flora cried as they got out of the car in front of the Aves Inn and one miles-long bar of late sunlight lit a fire in the Oriental poppies inside the hedge and made an improbable blue heaven of a stand of iris.

Denis saw to the decanting of the luggage, the transporting of which was taken over by a tall pink-faced porter in a farmer's smock. Halfway up the path with the two women, Robert turned back.

Denis had gotten into the car and closed the door. Robert said, "Before you're off—do you think in a town like this they'd have a place that does express film developing? I'd like to surprise Mrs. Wallace tomorrow with her pictures."

Denis found his gaze uncomfortably close and unsettlingly intent for such an unimportant business as the developing of film.

"I don't know, I'll find out and let you know if

there is such a place." Not given to nervous additions where none was necessary, he went on, "I should think that in a village knee-deep in tourists there'd be . . ."

"And, not only Mrs. Wallace. I was lucky enough to be on the spot when they were working over that Panner girl's body at the Imperial and got a dozen or so good shots."

Denis blinked and a muscle moved in his jaw. Some comment was called for. "Well, as you're not in the news photography line but several hundred cuts above . . . I suppose it's a sort of shorthand for future films, or scenes, these oddments you stumble on here and there? If you want I'll take the film along in case—"

"No, just find out for me. Speaking of oddments—weren't you staying at the Imperial?"

"Yes." Denis went a deep dark red from his forehead to his throat. "But I didn't want to spread blood all over a picnic—tends to spoil the taste of pâté and Parma ham. Sorry, I must be off, the garage closes at . . ." with a glance at his watch.

"Just one thing. I have a British driver's license and in case you think there might be a business of police questioning later, hotel guests there on the scene and so on, I'd prefer to take on Mrs. Wallace's gardens for her. If, that is, you found you'd be detained in any way." Hard and harsh and probably terribly unfair, but he didn't want dark dangerous puzzles riding in the Gaspard; driving it.

"They'd never let you have this car, not the Gold Star. Shall we wait for the police chase before you flash your driver's license?"

Still very much disturbed, Robert watched the Gaspard turn around and go back toward the town center.

And Denis said to himself, Well, I was going to get it over with right away, anyway.

Edgar Betters, back home that evening at his semi-detached in High Ham, was looking at the local segment of the evening television news with his wife when along with the story of the murder nearby a still picture of Lucetta Panner was shown, an alive and attractive Luce (in a photograph lent by her friend the beautician). He swallowed his lager the wrong way and doubled over in a fit of coughing. When he recovered, "Why, that's the girl in the bar last night, the poor stranded girl I told you I bought a drink for, she'd had a fight with this chap"—his eyes opened very wide—"and now she's dead, poor lass."

Mrs. Betters, the only negative excitement of whose life was her bad back, said, "Don't you think you should go to the police, or call them? Describe the man and that?"

"No . . . these aren't days you lift a finger without thinking twice. If I accused the wrong man, he might after the police got through with him come after me with a meat axe. Destruction of reputation and so on. No, let it be. But I do think you can bring me another lager.''

As—after unpacking and sharing a pot of tea with Flora—Emily went out of the inn to the gently lifting hill behind it, a short conversation about this present activity took place in her mind.

What are you doing wandering about at this hour?

Well, it's a lovely evening, and I thought that from a height I might get a distant view of Glastondel.

A view was more than she got: a kind of dream held in timeless suspension. The green parkland fell away beyond the yew hedge, its nobility of space defined by trees and water suggesting the hand of Capability Brown. The land rose again, softly, to a sort of plateau on which was set the solemnly graceful Georgian house, its front alabaster-white as the sun abruptly decided to sweep it. An almost perpendicular green hill rose immediately behind the house, and from it twin waterfalls fell on either side, probably from a stream deliberately divided in two. The waterfalls poured their white spirits into a wide oblong pool in front and descended in smaller falls down over an informal course of rocks, flowers, and elegantly trimmed dark cypresses to join the waters of the quiet lake to the left, under a line of century-old oak trees. Even from here, she thought she heard the elemental call of water. Overhead, to make the mysterious beauty even more piercing, a skylark sang.

She was so caught up in enchantment that she didn't hear the step behind her as she sat, arms around her knees, on the grass, and was startled when the tweed coat was thrown around her shoulders, the smell of him coming in a gust from it, the salty sea-grass smell.

"Two can play at that game," Robert said, sitting down beside her. "And in case you haven't noticed, it's getting chilly, Emily."

He took her near hand in his, looked at it thoughtfully, and kept it. "Hand's all right so far. Warm."

"Glastondel is—beaten-up word but literally so —lovely," Emily said, gazing ahead at the vision.

"Yes. I've seen it, and ten other gardens while in search of you."

Silence. In search of you? A younger man's memories to dip into; dip, refresh yourself, and go?

He too was looking directly ahead of him, as though he would lose his train of thought if he turned and looked into her face.

"I told you someone had told me you were thinking of marrying again. It got me on the telephone to New York. I won't bore you with all the people I had to talk to and all the trouble I had to take." Faintly amused complaint.

"Then, and now I will bore you—perhaps— but, the history of my travels. A hired car, not a Gaspard. I knew you were to start a swing south of London and was given your rough itinerary. I always seemed to arrive at a place after you'd left, and sometimes"—indignantly—"there were no guest books to be signed, no hint whatever. Anyway, garden after garden, plying binoculars and all but shouting your name to the rooks. In one place I caught an awful attack of some kind of pollen allergy and sneezed half the night . . ."

"In pursuit of exactly what?"

"Don't be obtuse, Emily, it's not one of your characteristics to be obtuse."

"All right." She looked down at her hand in his, but his clasp made the hand invisible. "To spend a few nights with me for old times' sake?"

"To spend a life with you, for old times' sake."

On astonishing cue, the skylark reappeared far overhead, flight and song, sun on its wings.

"Now I'm going to have to spell things out again. The old principle of wanting something you can't have and when you can have it finding out that after all . . . the matter of Vere. But I was so appalled, not for weeks or months, close to years, about what I'd done to you, to my Emily, to my own—"

The sound of his voice gave her a sweet sort of pain. She put her other hand on top of his. "Stop for a minute if you . . ."

"No. That ghastly good-natured bed of yours, that innocent bed tied up in ribbon so I could get a good night's sleep. And I thinking you had sent me a nest of adders to rest my head on." He was silent. He put an arm around her shoulders and turned to face her.

"Then when I heard—well, I had to get to you

198

before you got yourself really committed elsewhere.'' He kissed her, quietly and slowly, took his face a few inches away, looked into her eyes and again down to her marrow. ''You know perfectly well you can't marry anybody but me. At any time. Don't you, Emily?''

And then, ''For God's sake don't cry, darling, or so will I. And that would get in the way of . . .''

After a while, Emily said, ''Do you suppose people over there can see us?''

''What is there to see? A happy couple on a hillside, this grass is much too spiky to . . . and even in this permissive age, and even up under that spreading oak . . .''

Emily kissed the scarred eyebrow, her favorite eyebrow in all the world. ''Flora and I are sharing a room, the inn was pretty well filled up. She's rather formally inclined and thinks of me'' —Emily heard to her surprise her own laughter—''as a nice quiet woman and great reader, not a wanton slithering up hotel corridors at midnight.''

''Tomorrow will do. And after. Let no man put asunder, immediately following tonight. Come on, Emily, drinks, dinner, Flora.''

Getting up, lifted by his hand, Emily said, ''She'll be wondering where we are.''

''I don't think so. But we have to celebrate in any case—in our for the moment limited fashion.''

Five-thirty. Although, God, Betsy Yore thought, it might as well be midnight or near it, dark as it was outside, rain and low cloud and drifts of mist.

She hadn't been up this early since she'd had to dash off from London to her Aunt Clarissa's cremation in Hornbury five years ago. Always an early riser herself, her aunt had sternly prearranged this ceremony for eight o'clock in the morning.

She couldn't, as she was tempted to, throw herself together. She had to look fetchingly gotten up to meet her friend from Penzance, at Plymouth. Close-fitting white boucle suit, emerald-green silk blouse with a bow at the throat, green sandals to match, white hoop earrings, six white-and-gilt bracelets on one arm, and full makeup down to the green eye shadow.

She had, she found, brought her umbrella. And, Betsy thought, if I get spattered with mud and wet so what? My friend who isn't meeting me at Plymouth won't give a damn.

And the railway station was just across the street.

Her stomach was conditioned never even to think about breakfast until eleven or so, but a cup of tea would have come in handy. Maybe later, and not that much later.

Paying her bill at the desk, crossing the lobby, going out the door, and opening her umbrella, she was aware, the feeling a kind of flickering over her skin, of unseen eyes, watching her.

If she knew the Tickells of the world, and if she knew stark terror when she saw it, he would be at some window at a corridor's end above, making sure with his own eyes that she was going to board a down train, an early down train.

She climbed the wooden steps, cold in her finery, wishing she'd brought a warm coat, but if the trains ran on time in this out-of-the-way place, she wouldn't have long to wait.

The 6:14 came in right on time, all two cars of it. Betsy got on, noting that the station house wouldn't hide her, as the little train stopped short of it. Here I am, Tick, getting on the train, see?

She got off at the next stop, five miles away, Acreford. In a cafe on the platform, she took time to swallow a cup of hot sweet tea. A sense of hurry pressed nervously on her. If she were him, she'd want to do it early, get it over, and get out, whatever it was.

She saw down at the foot of the station steps a cab stand which held one lone gray car. The rain had stopped for the moment but the drifting mist made everything even more unreal. She opened the door and got into the cab. "Spill, please. The station cafe. I want to surprise a friend—does it have a side entrance, do you know, the cafe?"

Yes, it did, the driver said, because it was just beside the car park and it saved steps for people getting out of their cars, not having to go round by the front.

"If you'll drop me right up against the

cafe doorstep, please, I don't want to get spattered . . ."

"I wouldn't wonder, nice turnout like that," said her driver.

She slipped into the cafe, which was already busy and noisy with breakfasters, and found a place near but not at a front window where she could see the hotel entrance but could not, from it, be seen.

She ordered a cup of tea and—was it nervousness that made her stomach feel empty, hollow?—two currant buns.

It was now a few minutes after seven o'clock. Halfway through her cup of tea, and one bun consumed, Tickell emerged from the doorway of the Spill Arms.

Betsy had gone to the cash register when her breakfast was served and paid her bill, upon which the counter attendant scrawled a large X. She waved this at him as she flashed past the desk. To her left were rest rooms on a small hallway and at the end of the hall a half-curtained door opening on the car park.

Standing well back from the closed door, she watched Tickell sort his way through cars to where his motorcycle was parked at the rear of the big asphalt oblong.

He was no sooner on it, and proceeding at crawl pace through the cars, then out at the gate, when Betsy ran to her car, got into it, and started the engine.

Cycles were speedy things but she thought that

within the town limits he couldn't go roaring along at forbidden speeds—and calling all kinds of attention to himself while he was at it.

She swung out at the gate and gave thanks for two buses, one in front of Tickell, one behind, the road so narrow he couldn't curve out and pass the first, or not yet, because traffic was coming pretty steadily the other way.

In an effort to conceal herself a little, she pulled down the driver's sun shield. The first bus took a sharp right turning and now Tickell was relatively free to move; but signs at every corner said, "Speed limit 25 mph."

The town proper ended abruptly, meadows opening up on either side. Now there was only the one bus between them. The speed limit now specified was 35 mph.

At a signpost reading Spill Industrial Park and Xavier Road, the bus took the left fork. An impatient Bentley just behind Betsy passed her, for which she was briefly grateful, the motorcycle in front. But she didn't think the Bentley would stand aside for motorcycles. It didn't. It swept on and left Tickell and her, in her little green car, alone on the dark misty road with the cows on either side.

Betsy told herself in surprise that there was something safe-feeling in the presence of cows. Not that they'd go charging at anything, or protect you, but they looked so large and solid, so harmless and kind.

Approaching a bend in Xavier Road, she was

held up by a pickup truck loaded with untidy lumber coming out of a side lane. The sound of the motorcycle became fainter. Swearing, Betsy waited, then picked up speed, but the road, Xavier Road, was as bendy, in her mental phrase, as a sleeping snake, and when she passed a stand of sycamore trees there was nothing in sight, nothing at all.

Oh well, I'll cruise around a bit, Betsy thought. I might be able to pick up the sound of him before the sight of him.

The excitement of the hunt ran strongly through her veins. And if, as seemed not unlikely, she had lost the track and the scent, and the sound, she could catch up with him later, in London.

"Hi, Tick. Now we have even more odds and bits to chat about. Did you sell any motorbikes in Spill? And order me a champagne cocktail, will you?"

❦ ❦ EIGHTEEN

Denis had set his rising hour for six but did not choose to call the desk to ask them to wake him. He'd have to rely on his mental alarm clock, and alarm, he thought, was a good word at the moment.

Yesterday evening, after rejecting the idea of driving around for a preparatory look at the crossroads (the car was far too noticeable, it would be like setting yourself up in screaming headlines) he had taken the flawlessly performing Gaspard to Constable Bros. garage next door to the Tit-for-Tat Inn. The garage was large and clean and looked expensive; they ought to deliver a whopping bill for doing nothing, which was satisfactory, the bill to hand to Flora to exhibit the necessity for a side trip to Spill.

A fair man in blue coveralls all but sighed with joy as the Gaspard entered his wide-open red doors. "Oh God, oh I never," he said, and when

Denis stopped the car he came over and lovingly patted the shining plum bonnet.

"Will you—" Denis began, and paused at a phrase in the evening news broadcast coming from a radio in a corner.

". . . in connection with the case of the murdered brunette in Catchley, the police are anxious to contact a Mr. John Tickell, a close associate of Miss Panner's . . ."

Close associate my ass, Denis thought. By now they'd know he lived with her. And he would be missing from the flat—a man just out of the jug to boot—and he would be their luscious tempting first choice. And if they did get into touch with Tickell, the first thing he would offer them, damningly, was Denis Taunton.

These cogitations took perhaps a tenth of a second.

"Will you look her over thoroughly, plugs, bearings, the works?" he resumed. "These old dears will run like velvet and then all of a sudden, miles from nowhere—well, you know."

"There's nothing I'd like better," the mechanic said. "End of the day, you look a little . . . can I offer you a shot of something you fancy?"

"No thanks." Glastondel ought to occupy at least Flora's and Emily's morning. He thrust out of his mind any possible activities on Robert Marne's part. "Do you think you can have her ready and willing by say two o'clock?"

"I'll try." The mechanic also had a vision of his lovely bill.

Denis asked him if there was a place where express film developing could be done and was told that, yes, there was, and given the name and address.

Glad to be by himself, on his own, he went to a pub and spent a good two and a half hours drinking bitter and winding up with a plate of superb roast beef which he barely tasted.

He asked a man sitting next to him, "Is there a garage out at that crossroads east of town? Xavier, Orme, Enderby roads, I can't remember the other."

"Na, somebody put you wrong. There's nothing but an old burned-down place, Larkinses used to live there, donkeys' years back. Glastondel bought up all that property, acres around, so they wouldn't have soft-drink stands and roundabouts and that cluttering up the landscape."

When he returned to the inn on foot, he left a written message concerning his film to be given to Mr. Robert Marne.

Departing from his usual custom, he had booked himself into the Aves along with the others. The little round O near the crossroads lay approximately, according to his map, a little over half a mile north of the situation of the Aves Inn.

No color television sets here, either, but there was a radio built discreetly into the bed's headboard. Before getting into bed at midnight, he turned it on.

There was nothing at all on the news about Luce.

In reverse irritation close to bitterness, he thought, tempest in a teapot, good for a few lines while it's hot. But, just a bar girl from London . . . "probably no better than she should be."

He lay awake a long time, his mind overactive. Try to think of something pleasant. The idea about Emily—interesting, hopeful, amusing—had fizzled out twenty-four hours after Marne had made his appearance. So, nothing to think about in that direction.

Whether it was because of the darkness of the morning, or the fact that he had a light troubled sleep and hadn't really fallen deep in, his mental alarm went off late, six-fifteen.

He dressed quickly, dark pants, jersey, heavy-soled sneakers, quilted jacket, in the pockets of which were a neatly looped length of nylon rope he had taken from the boot of the Gaspard, and a handful of pitons. He thrust the hammer, also from the Gaspard's tool kit, slantwise through his belt in front. He went down and quietly through the little front lounge, nodding to the woman at the desk reading a book.

He was glad of the foul weather. Not a morning for early jaunts, or netting butterflies. He crossed the road and headed, over rising meadows, into the woods, going north, going fast.

Leo, paws on the low windowsill, was investigating the morning. Flora and Emily's room was on the second floor, facing the road, its windows just over the roof of a little tea pavilion jutting out at one side.

The mysterious wet smell, the country smell, was delicious to the poodle. His dark eyes roved eagerly. Then, to his wonder, for a moment against the horizon of a far hill, he saw a figure, a man, Denis.

He leaped out onto the roof of the pavilion. Flora, who had been half awake, seeing him at the window with semi-awareness, sat up and cried, "Emily!"

Emily shot upright in the other bed. "What . . . ?"

"Leo—he just jumped out the window—oh, *Emily,* and my ankle is still—oh, he'll be killed, make sure of that, a car, oh, my God—"

Outside, Leo took a look at the eight-foot drop to a bed of white alyssum and chanced it, and made it.

In the fourteen seconds she took to dress, seizing whatever was nearest, in the closet, Emily tried gaspingly to offer reassurance. "He's probably quite near . . . and just a quiet road outside . . . I'll call and he'll be right with us, you'll see . . ." and then she was out the door.

In spite of her confident promises, she had no idea of how to proceed after rushing down the brick path to the arch, and through it. First she stood still and shouted his name, five times, six. The road curved sharply to the right and again to the left. A bakery van went by at what seemed to her a terrifying speed. Was, somewhere in its wake, a dead or dying Leo?

Her voice was at screaming pitch now. "Leo, Leo, *Leo!*"

From far away, across the road, across the meadows, she head the unmistakable high crisp sound of a poodle bark. Was he answering? Or running after some wood animal? Or was it somebody else's poodle?

She crossed the road and began to run, through the fine rain and mist, toward the place where the bark might have come from.

Robert dreamed that he heard Emily screaming. He woke abruptly and then realized that it hadn't been a dream, that a real sound had pierced his sleep. Its imperative echoes still rang in his mind.

He never slept in pajamas and had to dress from the skin out, which took a little under a minute. He threw open his door so hard that it hit the wall with a bang which startled awake the Honorable Alexia Cather in the next room.

A door opened at the front end of the corridor as he was running to the stairway. Flora, clutching her bathrobe, said, "It's not Emily—"

"Not *Emily?*"

"I mean nothing's happened to her, she was screaming for Leo, he jumped out the window and ran away and I'm sure he'll be killed." Tears streamed down her cheeks. "Emily was calling him, or more than that, poor darling . . . first I thought she'd seen him dead in the road when I heard her and then I saw her take off into the field on the other side, running towards the woods.''

An immense relief swept Robert. ''I'll go help look. He's a biddable dog, Flora, he's probably just out for a romp.'' Seeing the day, the dark, the rain and mist, which he hadn't even noticed in his first panic, he took several seconds to go back to his room for his raincoat and then ran down the stairs and out.

Leo was lost.

He had run with all his heart and legs to where he had seen the figure against the sky, his ears flapping with the speed of his quest. When he reached the beginning of the woods, larch and birch, pine and young oak, he paused, looked, sniffed, and suddenly quivered with the damp and the cold, and disappointment, and a worried confusion.

He wandered into the woods and came to a stream. Running bands of water were new to him. He put a paw in, withdrew it, looked at the water, and uttered a furious bark of frustration and uncertainty, the bark that the wind carried to Emily.

He thought that from the far side of the water he heard, distantly, a sound of movement, a swishing of leaves. After a brief hesitation, he jumped into the water and swam the seven feet across, clambered up the flowery bank and violently shook himself. There was water in his eyes and nose and ears and a sniffling course on the leaf-covered floor of the woods here on this other side told him nothing, led him nowhere.

He shook his head again to clear his ears and stood, listening, lonely, lost.

What if Tickell chose to visit this interesting spot, which now couldn't be far ahead, at the same time as he, Denis, did?

His nerves strung tight, Denis stopped for a moment, leaned against a tree, and lit a cigarette for comfort and thought.

I'll tell him that Mrs. Wallace is interested in buying property in Spill—so near that beautiful Glastondel, you know—and she asked me to have a look at possible situations at the crossroads, where land could be purchased by persons of acceptable means and mien from the owners of Glastondel.

That ought to do it. He felt a grim smile lifting his mouth a little. He heeled out his cigarette and went steadily on.

At the burned-out house, its scene blessedly bathed in mist and silence, not a sound, not even a bird call, he saw the well and thought, the O, of course. He transferred the rope to his belt in front, and the pitons, which might or might not be necessary for the climb back up, into his right front pocket. The flash went into his left-hand pocket for the moment. He took off his jacket, rolled it up, and thrust it deep into a thick stand of lilies.

He removed the well cover and then, when he was inside, shoulders braced against, thank God, dry and not mossy rock, sneaker soles pressing hard and firm, knees doubled, reached up and pulled the cover almost back into place, so that to the casual or even interested eye it looked very little disturbed.

He switched on his flashlight, holding it in his mouth, because he needed both hands to inch down. In effect, he was chimneying; an art he had learned when at one time he had devoted three months to mountain climbing.

Down, down. Thirty feet, forty—where did the water begin? He swung his head forward to point the flash vertically. Another twenty feet at least, bringing up horrible cold visions of a Dantesque nature, end-of-the-world dark water, exit tunnel to doom.

It was just that he didn't like enclosed spaces. He took a long breath and while doing so his shoulders moved down to a patch of rock that was slippery with moss because of the nearness of the water.

He slid, tried to stop himself, and landed in the water, and with a sense of death darkening his mind, senses, and instincts found that his head wasn't even in it, he was standing up in only about five feet of water.

He stood still for a moment, getting his breath and his nerve back. Then he forced himself to investigate what was in the water with him.

A human skeleton, in a crumpled sprawl, head

down, what had been the feet up at a cocked angle. Denis got his hammer from his belt, and with the claw end ripped a hole in an imperishable plastic bag. In the gold light through the clear amber water he saw a glow of pearls, the reds and greens and blues of what might be and probably were rubies, emeralds, sapphires, and God knows what else.

The larger bag resting on top of part of the skeleton had rotted on one side. He plunged in a hand and took out a heavy cup which had been lodged in the branches of a candelabra. By their weight and glisten and color, both objects announced themselves unmistakably as gold. He ran a hand deeper into the rotted bag. Coins, pounds of them, something that felt like a chalice, long stem on it anyway, a jumble of smaller stuff, rings, bracelets . . . all of it gold.

The thought flashed across his mind that it was like an old-fashioned and crudely done allegory—the skeleton, the gold and jewels.

The light in the well changed in a sudden and remarkable way, even this far down. He looked up and saw the well cover vanish, the circle of what, gray as it was, seemed daylight brilliance, and then the light blocked partially as a man's body carefully and slowly entered the well, hands holding onto a rope.

The body began its descent. Denis made a small involuntary noise, a fate-taken animal noise. A flashlight was directed down at him.

Tickell, at the sight of the man below, almost

let go of the rope. Now wait, now wait, he counseled his pounding heart and pulses, he's below and I'm above, I hold every card, nothing to be afraid of.

He didn't think he wanted another murder on his hands, one was one too many, considering. The thing to do was stun the man, put him out of action, get the hell out of this, get the hell out of everything, forget Yore and his treasure in the well.

He had his knife on him but he couldn't aim accurately at say a shoulder or a wrist from this height, in this tight space. The thing to do was crawl up and out and get something heavy, a rock, heave it down and run.

Leo in his distraught ramblings came upon, at the foot of a tree, a smell and an object that he recognized with alert passion, a cigarette end that proclaimed Denis to him. From not far behind, in the woods, he heard Emily's voice crying, "Leo, Leo," the voice hoarse now, tears in it.

He plunged forward, having picked up Denis's body scent. He arrived at the well just as Tickell was getting himself out of it and began a tremendous spurt of barking.

"For Christ's sake get away from me!" ordered Tickell, who was frightened of unleashed dogs. Emily followed the sound of the barking and emerging from the willows saw the man, searching the ground, then coming up with a thick round length of blackened wood that looked as if it might at some time have been part of a porch pillar.

Denis, living in minutes the greatest terror he had ever felt, expecting a bullet, expecting death, heard Leo and bellowed, *"Watch out,"* whether to Leo or to whomever might be with him he didn't know.

Emily swooped toward Leo with unbelieving joy but the man dropped his piece of pillar and snatched up the poodle before she could reach him.

"Get the hell out of here," he said. "Or, down the well with the dog."

She used the last vestiges of her voice to scream, not a name, not "Leo," just a scream.

Robert, raincoat flying, came around a stand of Norway firs and bent and picked up the heavy round of wood. He struck from behind, hard on Tickell's shoulder. Tickell dropped Leo with a shout of pain, turned and saw the man, saw he was outnumbered, saw he was finished. Or almost. Unless—

He had hidden his motorcycle in the trees on the other side of the drive. No time for that.

He got out his knife and held it viciously blade forward to the man and the woman and the dog. "After me and you'll get this," he gasped, and turned and ran down the drive and into the road.

Run, run, catch a lift with luck in a few minutes—"My car broke down, can you take me along wherever you're headed and drop me off at a garage?" The police wanted, as he had heard on

216

the radio, to talk to a John Tickell, but he wasn't Tickell, he was Ernest Dawson the brown-haired chap.

About eighty yards down Gulliver Road a green Subaru pulled up beside him and stopped. Betsy Yore leaned out of the window, with her Beretta held firmly in her hand.

"Poor old Tick, you're bleeding like a pig. Can I give you a lift anywhere? Get in the car, do. But first, drop that knife on the road."

Tickell looked at the automatic, dropped the knife, and went around and got into the car.

After a time he couldn't measure, he asked faintly, "Where are we going?"

"To look at cows and things, take our time, talk," Betsy said. "I'd first thought I might drive you straight to the police station. I hear they're looking for you, to talk to you."

Kill our Al, will you?

"But, I thought, what's in that for me? Nothing but my name in the records, handing somebody in. I don't work for nothing—particularly for the police."

She glanced over at him. "Haven't you a handkerchief to mop up some of that blood? It's running from your hand right onto the seat, but I suppose with this vinyl—Well, to get back to our talk, Al isn't really alive as far as I know. Dead—and probably to put it politely as far as *you* know. What I thought was this. I've had a tough life in many ways and I'm not getting any younger. A nice little monthly income for the rest of my life wouldn't hurt. From you. You'd have to scurry for it, as you said, but . . ."

"Is that gun loaded?" Voice still faint.

"Take my word for it, yes."

He sighed and said, "Will I be executed if I have a cigarette?"

"No. Go ahead."

He took the battered pack out of the breast pocket of his shirt, lit a match, and then reached over and held the match flame to her thumb.

Betsy snatched away her hand to put the scorched thumb to her mouth.

With the skilled speed of the committed, he picked up the automatic.

Ernest Dawson very quickly shot John Tickell through the head.

The publishers hope that this Large Print Book has brought you pleasurable reading. Each title is designed to make the text as easy to see as possible. G. K. Hall Large Print Books are available from your library and your local bookstore. Or you can receive information on upcoming and current Large Print Books and order directly from the publisher. Just send your name and address to:

G. K. Hall & Co.
70 Lincoln Street
Boston, Mass. 02111

or call, toll-free:

1-800-343-2806

A note on the text
Large Print edition designed by
Bernadette Strickland.
Composed in 16 pt English Times
on an Editwriter 7700
by Debra Nelson of G. K. Hall Corp.